JAVA
JACK

Luqman Keele

Daniel Pinkwater

THOMAS Y. CROWELL   NEW YORK

JAVA
JACK

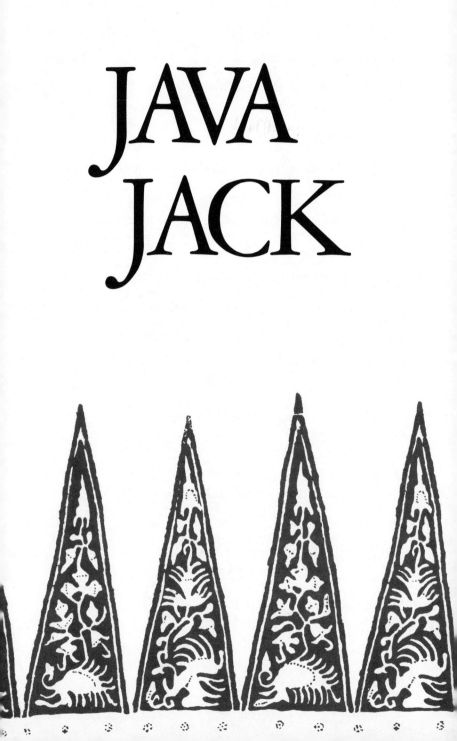

Library of Congress Cataloging in Publication Data
Keele, Luqman.
Java Jack.
SUMMARY: When Jack travels to the Indonesian
island of Maggasang to search for his missing
anthropologist parents, he begins a series of
incredible adventures which take him outside the
universe.
[1. Adventure stories. 2. Space and time—
Fiction] I. Pinkwater, Daniel Manus, 1941–
joint author. II. Title.
PZ7.K2258Jav   [Fic]   79-7892
ISBN 0-690-03995-6
ISBN 0-690-03996-4 lib. bdg.

10 9 8 7 6 5 4 3 2 1
First Edition

For Sahlan

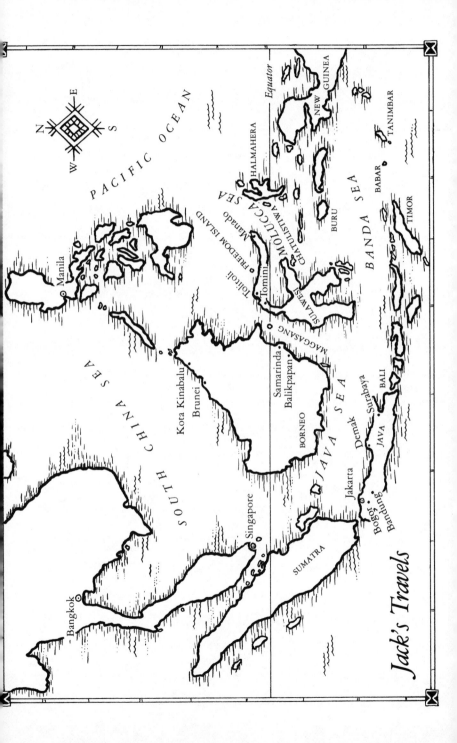

Jack's Travels

1 IT'S NOT THAT I dislike the other kids, it's just that ever since I was sent to Neosho and entered the first grade a year older than the other kids, everybody picked on me for looking different. I just got used to ignoring it. Still, I'm not your average kid. For one thing, I have blond hair and black skin. It's not really black, but close enough for the other kids in town to call me nigger. The blond hair must confuse them. And my face is sort of Asian or maybe Hawaiian looking. I don't look anything like either of my parents.

But there's more that isn't average about me. For example, I know how to fly. That's something the other kids don't know. There's this guy, Charlie—he's a friend of my Aunt Amy. Charlie belongs to a club of guys, mostly retired Army and Air Force types, who like to fool with vintage airplanes. They have a place out near Camp Crowder. Charlie has a fully restored B–17, and I've flown it lots of times. I've flown small planes too. I have more than a thousand hours of flying logged, and that doesn't count the flying I've done outside the country.

Another thing that's not average for Neosho, Missouri, where I live with my Aunt Amy, is that I was born in Java. I lived there until my parents decided that it was time for me to go to school in the States, and sent me here.

The rest of the kids in Neosho are very average. They take pride in it. Maybe if I told them about the flying, they'd feel like being friends with me in the hope of getting a free ride—but I've just never felt like telling them. I've never told them about things I've seen and done in Java, either. And I've never told them about my room.

My room is probably the most unaverage place in this town. I have all the stuff my folks sent me from Maggasang, Borneo, Java, New Guinea, and Bali. It's all hanging on the walls, cluttering up the tables, and littering the floor. There are batik cloths in brown, yellow, red —all colors—and dark blue ones with swirling curlicue designs pinned up everywhere and spread over the bed and chairs. I have my tiger's head hung over the door, my Dyak spears on the closet door, and my wavy-blade kris knives on wires hanging from the ceiling. My stuffed mouse deer is on one side of my TV, and my stuffed weebo "rabbit" sits on the other side. The TV itself is inside a red and gold carved chest with Garuda birds for legs. It adds something to late movies to watch them framed by that Balinese chest. On top of the TV chest is a picture of my parents.

Maggasang, that's where they'd gone after sending me to Aunt Amy. That's where they thought it might be too rough on a kid, living back in the jungles with them. I

had some copies of *National Geographic* and similar maga-
zines with articles about my parents, or by them. There'd
be a picture of my father with an orangutan slung around
his neck and a bunch of natives standing around smiling.
His name is Jeff Robinson, my mother is Marie—and I'm
Jack, only I wasn't with them. I wasn't in Maggasang—
I was in Neosho, Missouri, where I didn't belong.

Living with Aunt Amy wasn't bad—far from it. I really
loved her, and she loved me. I'd been living with her for
about half my life. And, except that nobody my age ever
talked to me, living in Neosho wasn't really bad either.
For one thing, there was Charlie, and the flying, which
I really liked. I mean both, Charlie and the flying. And
I got letters and neat presents from my folks. The day
would come when I'd go out to Maggasang—or wherever in the world they were—and help them. I'd be a
bush pilot, and fly supplies in and out of camp.

Even before that, I was supposed to see them for a
whole summer. This had been decided ahead of time,
and then a letter arrived with the airline tickets and in-
structions to get myself a passport and come on out the
day school was over.

Getting a passport and the necessary visas can be pretty
complicated and take a lot of time if you do it from
Neosho. So I talked Charlie into flying up to Joplin with
me where we could have it all processed in an afternoon.
Charlie suggested we make a weekend of it and, after we
finished up in Joplin, fly down to Noel, a little town by
a lake in the Ozark foothills.

We didn't take the B–17. Charlie also had an old Cessna, and we went in that. We flew to Powers Airfield, which is right beside Lake Noel. We came in at dusk. Everything looked really pretty, twinkling with strings of lights along the boardwalk, all dotted with waffle stands and ice cream wagons. The colored lights reflected in the lake water along with the rainbow colors of the sunset. It reminded me of the story Aunt Amy had told me about the lake.

It was a legend about the Pawnee Indians who lived on the shores of the lake long ago. The lake was the property of a giant Indian nobody could see. He was called the Invisible Hunter. He always came across the lake at sunset, and the Indians could hear him, hear the sound of his canoe paddle, and they could see the prints of his big moccasins in the sand, but they never saw him.

The story went that the only one ever to see him was this one girl who was so plain and unimportant that nobody ever paid the slightest bit of attention to her. It was sort of a Cinderella story. The girl finally got to see the Invisible Hunter, and he turned out to be fifteen feet tall, and he had a bow and arrow. The bow was a rainbow, the arrow was a golden comet, and the bowstring was all the stars in the Milky Way.

Coming into Noel that evening, I remembered the story, and felt as if it were really true.

We stayed over at the Noel Motel, and left the next day, right after breakfast. The passport and visas arrived in Neosho, Special Delivery, a few days later—about an hour before the news came that my parents were missing, and probably dead.

 2   IT CAME OVER the TV news: "American anthropology team Doctors Jeff and Marie Robinson have been reported missing in the jungles of Maggasang, a tiny tropical island in the territorial waters of Indonesia. Sources report the likelihood that the Robinsons are the most recent victims of a headhunting revival among the island's primitive Sea Dyak tribes."

Then there was a crackly long-distance call from someone named Mr. Sparrow. We couldn't make out whether he was with the U.S. government, or the Indonesian government, or some kind of associate of my parents. He said not to worry too much, that no definite information had come in yet, but that I should get to Maggasang as soon as possible. He said the airlines would be informed about me, and all arrangements would be made. He was going to meet me at the other end.

Things happened so fast that there wasn't really any time to think. Aunt Amy didn't say anything about it, and neither did Charlie—neither did I. None of us said anything about my going out to Maggasang fast so I could be present for my mother's and father's funeral.

I didn't cry. I wasn't sad, or scared, or much of anything—just sort of numb. Charlie flew me up to Kansas City, and I caught a plane for California with my round-trip ticket. I had about sixty dollars in cash, a traveler's check for a hundred, my passport and visas, and a small bag with some clothes in it. The airline had my name on some kind of a list, and they saw to it that I made my connections.

I had traveled by myself before—all the way from Java to Neosho when I was only seven years old. There's nothing to it really, just waiting around airports and getting on and off planes.

By the time I got to Tokyo, it was almost midnight—which is the same as nine in the morning the day before in Neosho. There was some kind of trouble at the airport—a demonstration, I think, with police and crowds with signs and torches. The airline people told us it would be dangerous to stay in a hotel out by the airport, so they were going to take us in to the city on a bus.

When you travel on international flights, if you have to stay in a place overnight, or more than a couple of hours, they give you a free room. I was sort of mixed up and tired from all the hours of flying and waiting, not to mention that I was still feeling sort of shocked and numb, so I was glad of the chance to go to bed for a few hours.

A lady from the airline found me on the bus and told me that I'd be picked up the next morning, and that I was entitled to a free breakfast at the hotel, the Ginza Capitalist—funny name for a hotel. Lots of things in Japan have funny names in English that don't quite fit, like Alabama Cleaners and Laundry, or Prince Sylvia Headcutters, which turned out to be a barber shop. I guess they just pick the name they like, never mind what it means.

My room at the Ginza Capitalist was more like a long closet. Everything in the room seemed to be made out of one piece of plastic. It was sort of like a ship's cabin, with the bed built into the wall, a one-piece bathroom, and just enough room to stand up in.

I slept pretty well, considering what was on my mind. When I woke up, the phone was ringing. I had some trouble finding it, because it was built into the bed, while the bell was built into the ceiling or the wall. Finally I located the thing, and picked up the receiver.

"Good morning, Mr. Robinson," a guy said at the other end. "You don't know me. I'm a reporter from the *Straits of Borneo Times.* I'd like to interview you about the death of your parents."

An awful way to wake up. I tried to collect my thoughts. "Are you . . . uh . . . Is it certain that my parents are really dead?"

"For sure. We just got word that their heads have been brought in."

I didn't like this guy. I decided not to believe him. If it were true, wouldn't someone from the airline have told me, or Mr. Sparrow? "How do you know that?" I asked.

"We've got a wiretap on the line from Government House in Maggasang. That's how we know where you are—they called your aunt in the States last night."

"That's spying!" I said.

"That's journalism," the guy on the telephone said. "Now, what about that interview? I'll treat you to breakfast."

I really hated this guy because of the crummy way he had told me that my parents were dead. I wanted to tell him to drop dead himself. Instead, I said that I was getting a free breakfast from the airline, and besides I didn't want to talk to anybody until I got to Maggasang and found out what had really happened.

"That's *if* you get to Maggasang, kid," the guy said in a nasty voice, and hung up. What a creep. I was mad. I wasn't going to believe some creepy crud from any newspaper who called me up and said my parents were dead. Just the same, I started crying, sitting in my one-piece plastic bed.

After a while, I pulled myself together and started getting dressed. There was a TV built into the wall, and I idly switched it on.

The program was in English, with Japanese subtitles. The announcer had an English accent. He was telling about a bunch of famous scientists who had mysteriously disappeared. It sort of caught my attention. My folks had disappeared too, though they were anthropologists, not space scientists. The guy went on to talk about the possibility that a new way to get to other worlds had been discovered—not by rockets, but some new secret way. I switched off the set, finished packing my bag, and went down to breakfast.

I don't get caught up in rumors easily. Aunt Amy made a point of educating me that way. She had been involved in a lot of strange stuff, like faith healing, and she said it was important to use your head. Just because someone was a professor, or said he was, and told you that spacemen built the pyramids, was no reason to believe it. People with brains waited for proof, she always said. That's what brains were for. That's why I wasn't going to believe the creep from the *Straits of Borneo Times*—

although, in spite of everything, I was afraid he was telling the truth.

Prices are high in Japan. I figured that my breakfast, if I had had to pay for it myself, would have cost me ten dollars. It wasn't much of a breakfast, either—everything looked and tasted like miniature toy food. While I ate, I was sort of looking around for the *Straits of Borneo Times* man. He was the type who would show up even when I had told him I didn't want to talk.

There was a guy who was watching me from behind a big Japanese picture magazine. On the cover was a color shot of the surface of Mars. The guy had skin so smooth that I would have been willing to believe he was a Martian himself. When he turned his face, I saw that he had a slithery scar that ran all the way from his forehead down beside his eye, across his cheek, and under his chin. It gave him a scary look, especially along with that smooth skin.

He caught me staring at him, and smiled at me. He had a set of absolutely perfect teeth. They looked like pearls. "Please allow me to say that I'm very sorry about your parents, Jack," the smooth guy said. Someone else knew who I was!

He put out his hand. He had long, slender fingers and pale beige skin. There wasn't a vein or a hair on his hand, just the tail end of some complicated tattoo. I couldn't tell what the picture was.

"May I present myself?" the smooth guy said. He handed me a business card that was the same color as his hand.

F.L.I.G.H.
The Fight for the Liberation of the Island of
Gunungan Heaven
c/o Free Island Movement
P.O. Box 748
Stockholm, Sweden

"If there is ever anything I can do for you," smooth Mr. Fligh said, and smiled his pearly smile. He scared me, like a snake. I was trying to say something polite to him—after all, it wasn't his fault that he was scary to look at—when I was called to the lobby to catch the airport bus. A little guy ran in and said, "Please hurry, Mr. Robinson, bus is leaving!" I grabbed my bag and dashed out. I was glad to get away from Fligh, but when I was on the bus, I saw that he had followed me out. He was standing there, watching the bus leave.

 3 THE PORTERS IN the Jakarta airport were all kids around my age. They were leaning on the railings and racks for luggage, and smoking fat cigarettes.

It's those clove cigarettes that give Indonesia its smell. The instant you step out the door of the airplane into the hot thick air, you smell them. They're called *kreteks,* meaning firecrackers, because they give off little explosions when you smoke them, and they crackle. You've got to take a drag and then hold the butt away from you so that the burning ashes don't fall on your shirt or trousers. All the porters had lots of little burn holes in their clothes.

Nobody met me or guided me the way they had done in the States and Tokyo. I was sweating, standing there waiting for my bag to come off the plane. My ticket said I had to catch another plane to Surabaya and then another to Samarinda in Kalimantan (that's Indonesian for Borneo), and then a final plane to Maggasang. I had maybe two more days of traveling ahead of me. The flight I'd taken in Tokyo had stopped in Osaka, Taipei, Hong Kong, Bangkok, and Singapore before finally getting in to Jakarta, Indonesia. It had taken seventeen hours, including stopovers.

I went to the Merapi Airlines counter and asked them about my flight to Surabaya. They told me I had to go to another airport to catch it, but I'd never make it because it was clear across town. The guy at the counter suggested that I spend the night in Jakarta and try for a plane in the morning. I told him I had a whole series of planes to catch, but he said that most of them would probably be late anyway, hours and hours late.

I began to wonder if the guy from the *Straits of Borneo Times* had been right—maybe I'd never make it to Maggasang.

Maggasang is an island located in the deep straits between Kalimantan and Sulawesi—Sulawesi's the wishbone-shaped island they used to call the Celebes. If you look at it on a map, you can see that the shortest way to get there, coming from Tokyo, would be from Hong

Kong or Manila—except that there's no plane to Maggasang from those places. Singapore looks like the next best jumping-off place, but from there you have to go to Brunei, and from Brunei to Samarinda, *if* there's a plane, and sometimes there isn't. A lady in the airport in Tokyo had told me all this.

So I sat down in the airport in Jakarta to think things over. One of the porters offered me a cigarette. I don't usually smoke, but I took it, just for something to do. I accepted a light for the *kretek* and inhaled. It took two whiffs and I was high. The clove flavor covers up something mixed in with the tobacco, but I didn't know that then. I just felt like I was walking on cushion shoes and my bag didn't weigh anything. In this state I wandered around the airport for an hour or two, looking for someone who knew who I was, or who could help me figure out my next move.

Nobody seemed very anxious to help, and I finally decided I might as well try to find a hotel. I got into a taxi.

"Hey, mister!" The taxi driver spoke some English—that was good. I was still sort of high. "Hey, mister, you want to go to Surabaya?"

"Huh? Uh, yes . . . I mean, no. . . . I want a hotel."

"I take you to Surabaya, mister . . . only twelve hours. I drive like hell. All night. You sleep. You pay me fifty dollars. Cheap."

"I've got a plane ticket," I said.

"Good! You cash in ticket in Surabaya. Make money. You want to go?"

I nodded yes. The driver took off like a madman. I looked out the windows at water buffalos pulling big carts. The roadside was lined with palm trees. It all looked sort of familiar. I'd been in Jakarta before, but that was when I was very small. I recognized the big freedom monument—it's sort of like the Washington Monument with a golden flame on top.

We got out of the suburbs. The taxi was a 1958 Chevy, and it rattled and shook. The speedometer was reading a steady ninety-five. Either the guy was a good driver or the dial was broken, because the needle never moved. We tore along the narrow road to Bogor and up over the mountain pass to the central plain of West Java. The wind smelled of cloves and flowers, and the moon shone down on volcanos and rice fields. It had been more than half my life since I'd seen any of this, but it felt like home— more than Neosho, Missouri, ever had. In the back seat of the speeding taxi I fell asleep.

 4 I USED UP my last cash dollars to pay the taxi driver, whose name was Affandi. It was fifty dollars for the trip, and eight dollars for a new thirdhand tire, because he blew one out on the last stretch, between Demak and Surabaya, and didn't have a spare. We'd taken the north coast of Java route. After we got away from the big volcanos near Bandung, in the middle of Java, the terrain was flat and dull—a lot of moonlight on rice paddies along a whole lot of Java Sea.

The plane to Samarinda was overbooked, and there were people on standby waiting to squeeze on. There wasn't a chance I'd get a seat. Again, nobody had been informed that I was coming. The V.I.P. treatment had stopped in Tokyo, and I was on my own. And stuck in another airport. And broke. Nobody knew how to cash my traveler's check, and the little Bank Dabumi office in the airport never opened the whole day I was there.

I watched the buffalos wander across the runway, and the buffalo boys chasing after them, horsing around with bamboo poles. It was all familiar to me. I watched the Indonesian people in the airport. The place was fairly crowded, although there weren't many planes around, and none taking off or landing for long stretches of time. There were ladies with big behinds and big fronts wearing batik skirts all pleated in front, and tight-fitting orange or turquoise or purple blouses, and lots of jingly gold jewelry. There were men with safari suits made out of tweed or shiny synthetic stuff, wearing thick black glasses and squat black hats and smoking *kreteks* one after another.

There was one family of about fifteen people, and they were all carrying bamboo and rattan baskets and boxes stuffed full of horny fruit and bananas of all different shapes. They camped in the airport.

At first I thought they'd missed their plane, but then I heard they were waiting to catch a plane that was due to take off for Mecca in three or four days' time. They were getting ready. The fruit and stuff was to eat while they were waiting. They gave me a piece of horny fruit. I didn't remember it at first, but then I did—it smells awful, like a mixture of cheap Ozark molasses and throw-up. At least it was something to eat.

It got dark. I still sat there. It looked as though I might be there for a while, so I stretched out on a bench.

I woke up with two big hefty Indonesian guys poking me. They were wearing uniforms, and had dark glasses, and had medals and gold braid all over them. I sat up and lifted my legs out of the slats they'd got caught in.

"Are you the boy who wants to go to Maggasang?" The bigger man smiled at me. "We can cash your traveler's check, and we are flying to Maggasang now, if you want to go." He had a row of gold teeth. "I'm Captain Suryo," he said, "and this is Lieutenant Charma."

"How do you do?" I answered. I tried to wake up and get myself out of the bench I was tangled up with, and I fished around in my jeans for the traveler's check. "I've got a hundred-dollar traveler's check," I said. "Will that be all right?"

The two big Indonesians roared with laughter, as if what I'd said was a big joke. They whacked me on the back and picked up my bag and gently pushed me out the teak-framed doors onto the runway. The big family waved good-bye. I waved back.

I wanted to get straight what was happening—was I paying for my ride, or were these guys giving me a lift, or had they been sent out to get me?

The two fliers didn't want to answer any questions. They just wanted to laugh and slap me and each other on the back. They were friendly, there was no mistake about that.

The only plane on the field was a B–17, just like Charlie's—except his was all restored and neat and shiny. This one looked as though it had been flying without any repairs, or even a cleanup, since the end of World War II. We climbed in. The two fliers told me I could lie down in the back or sit up front with them. There weren't any seats in the cargo compartment, just a bunch of big green military-type duffel bags. They might have made a pretty good bed, but there was a stink of horny fruit and other garbage back there that made me decide to sit up front in the cabin.

We took off without any clearance from the tower. Suryo and Charma started eating as soon as we were off the ground. They shared their fried chicken and hot green peppers with me. The peppers have a delayed action. First you eat one, and think it tastes pretty good —then a minute later your mouth catches fire. They gave me some lukewarm tea from a thermos to soothe the pepper burn.

They were in no hurry about anything. They circled around over Surabaya twice so I could see the harbor and the Bugis boats—prahus, they're called—and the *Toriana,* a pretty white cruise ship that sails from island to island in the seas of Indonesia.

"Nice casino on the *Toriana,*" Suryo chortled.

"Jack, you want to fly the plane?" Charma said. He'd noticed me watching him closely during takeoff. He'd skipped a lot of the safety-first steps Charlie had taught me.

I hadn't said anything about knowing how to fly or having piloted a '17 just like this one. "Yeah, I'd like to see how it feels," I said. I changed seats with Suryo and settled in beside Charma. He smelled of cloves and spices. Sweat glistened all over his face. He and Suryo were winking and mugging at each other. I guess they expected me to chicken out. I kind of hesitated and then reached for the controls.

I checked a few gauges, picked up the airspeed a little, and put the old bomber into a gentle climb. I tried banking this way and that. The plane was old and crummy, but it handled just like Charlie's. I felt right at home. Suryo and Charma were looking at each other, amazed. I was having a hard time not breaking out laughing—their mouths were hanging open and their eyes were bugging out.

Then I went into the trick Charlie had shown me. You can't do fancy flips in a big airplane, but you can still do some pretty impressive things. I went into a slow banking turn, dipping the right wing all the way down so it pointed at the sea and the plane seemed to pivot on the wing tip, and chicken and garbage and cargo all went sloshing to the side.

When I leveled off and got back on our original course, Suryo and Charma were going crazy. "Boy can fly!" they shouted, and pounded me on the back. If there had been any chance they were going to take my traveler's check in return for the ride, that was now forgotten. They carried on for about fifteen minutes. After the excitement died down, they left me to fly the airplane and settled in the rear of the cabin to play a game of cards.

The old airplane handled beautifully, and it was a perfect flying night, clear and starry. You could see for miles and miles.

We'd taken off at about ten-thirty at night. At twelve midnight, I heard two heavy thuds behind me. I turned and looked back.

Suryo and Charma were lying on the cabin floor with ugly bloody wounds on their heads. I couldn't tell if they were dead or alive.

In between them stood a young man wearing a frayed fake-leather jacket painted with the letters F.I.M. I looked at his face. It was wrapped in a black scarf with holes cut out for the eyes.

He held his pistol relaxed in his right hand. A policeman's stick hung from his left wrist. He jerked his wrist and flipped the baton into "ready" position. I figured I was finished. I was too frightened to shake. I just turned around in my seat and took the controls again, looking at the stars, waiting for the blow to fall as it had on Suryo and Charma.

It seemed like a long time went by. "It's a pity you didn't accept my invitation to breakfast," said the voice of the *Straits of Borneo Times* man. I jumped in my seat—I'd had a feeling that guy was going to make trouble for me. "It's also a pity that you didn't have time to talk to me *after* breakfast," another voice said. This time it was Fligh, the smooth weird guy in the hotel.

I spun around in my seat. Fligh was alone; he'd taken his hood off. His pearly teeth gleamed—glowed, actually —in the dim light of the cabin. "Yes, I'm the man from the newspaper, and a few others—don't look so puzzled," he said in yet another voice, which was familiar, but I couldn't place it. "I have a number of voices. Don't you remember Mr. Sparrow?"

Mr. Sparrow! The guy who had telephoned for me to come out to Maggasang!

"What are you going to do with them?" I asked, looking at the bodies of Suryo and Charma. They weren't dead—I could hear them breathing.

"We're going to dump them out," Fligh said, smiling.

"No! Don't dump them out, please!" I shouted.

" 'Don't dump them out, pleeeease!' " Fligh mimicked my high-pitched squawk. "Why not? Why not dump the guys who dumped on your mother and father?"

"What do you mean?" I shouted. Then I noticed that Fligh was not alone. There were dark figures moving up from the cargo hold.

"I mean that these men are not your friends," Fligh said. "*We* are your true friends, although you don't know it yet. These two," he said, kicking the unconscious bodies of Suryo and Charma, "were sent out to kill you. But since you want us to spare their lives, we will—they can always get revolutionary justice later. Now let me introduce you to your real friends."

All this was said in as strange and sly and spooky a manner as you can imagine. I wasn't able to tell if Fligh was mocking me, or lying to me, or simply telling the truth, although in a really weird and unpleasant way.

"This is Borneo Bill," Fligh said, "your new brother."

I didn't understand any of this, but the more I saw and heard, the more I was sure that I should just be quiet and act pleasant. Borneo Bill was something like a big one-eyed loaf of speckled bread. He was holding a machine gun and wearing a jacket like Fligh's with F.I.M. painted on it and the arms cut off. F.I.M.—Free Island Movement, it had said on Fligh's card.

"And this is our sister, Sulawesi Sue," Fligh said. Borneo Bill hadn't said anything to me, but Sulawesi Sue wanted to talk. She was a pimply sallow-faced girl with long braids and a Mao jacket with the F.I.M. symbol.

"Sue Chen Wah from Sulawesi, my name," she said in a deep voice. She had a gun too.

"And this is Tolitoli Tommy, otherwise known as Timor Tim, or just T.T."

T.T. was a grisly character with long curly oily hair. He was a shrimp, about five inches shorter than me. "Hi! What's your handle, kid?" he said.

"Yah, Fligh—what do we call the kid?" Borneo Bill spoke at last. He had a slow, deep voice. He sounded as stupid as he looked, and as mean.

"It all depends on whether 'the kid,' as you call him, decides to join us or not," Fligh said.

"Where'd you come from?" I asked. "And what do you know about my folks?"

"If you mean where have we just now come from," Fligh said, "we were all in duffel bags in the back of the plane. And about your folks—well, they—that is, your father and mother—they were great personal friends of mine. And they were more than that. They were great revolutionary heroes. Before they were murdered."

My head was swimming. This creep was positively delighted telling me—for the second time, if you counted his impersonation of the newspaper guy—that my parents were dead. I didn't know if I should believe anything he said—but looking at all the guns, I knew I'd better pretend to believe him.

"Murdered! Who murdered them?" I shouted. "And how do you know all this?"

Fligh gestured with the muzzle of his gun at Suryo and Charma, who were in the process of being tied up. "Maybe not these very two," he said, "but they, or someone like them, had your parents killed."

"Why should I believe you?" I asked.

"Because I have proof," Fligh said. He handed me a color Polaroid photograph of a dark brown native holding two ugly shrunken heads.

I almost fainted.

Mother's ash blond hair was streaked with mud, and Father's gray-brown beard had twigs and dead leaves tangled in it. The faces were all pinched and brown. If those were really their faces. You couldn't tell.

"I took this picture yesterday in Maggasang," Fligh said. "They are your parents' heads."

Yesterday he was in Tokyo with *me*! I couldn't figure

out why, but this guy was going to a lot of trouble to convince me that my parents were dead, and I thought I'd better play along. My shock at seeing the picture was wearing off, but I didn't let on. I took the opportunity to handle the plane badly, as if I were sort of half crazy with grief, and nobody tried to take over the controls. That suggested that nobody there knew how to fly, and I was pretty safe from getting killed, at least while we were in the air. Of course, there was the possibility that none of these guys had figured all this out. Borneo Bill and Sulawesi Sue, especially, looked as if they'd shoot me first and then figure out that there was nobody to fly the airplane.

"I know you're confused at this moment," Fligh said, "but please understand that the same people who killed your parents are the people we are organized to fight. By joining us you will serve a great cause, and also have revenge on the murderers of your mother and father."

"And if you're not with us, you're against us," said Borneo Bill.

"And you die!" said Sulawesi Sue.

I decided to join the movement.

Fligh pulled out a funny-shaped medallion hanging on a chain. He held the necklace in one hand and the Polaroid picture in the other. Borneo Bill unbuttoned his shirt and pulled out a similar medallion, and Sulawesi Sue leaned over and hers popped out of her jacket, and T.T. held out his wrist at me.

Each of them had one, and each was different, shaped like the island that each person was named after. I recog-

nized the wishbone shape of Sulawesi, the dog's head of
Kalimantan Borneo, and the fishtail of Timor.

The medal Fligh was holding out to me was in the
shape of the island of Java. "Sign this paper and you're
one of us, Java Jack," he said.

I hesitated.

"How come he not sign?" Sulawesi Sue asked. "Fligh,
he not sign, we throw him out, and the soldier boys too."

Fligh's smooth face showed no expression, but something in his look seemed to plead with me to make it easy
on myself.

The F.I.M. kids were shouting "New revolutionary
brother!" and "Three cheers!" as I signed and became
Java Jack.

 5 FLIGH STUCK THE Polaroid picture to
the window. It clung to the moisture on
the glass. He hung the medallion from
the compass so it dangled in front of my
nose. "This is our new course," he said,
handing me a scrap of paper.

We didn't go to Maggasang. We came near it. I could
see the cloud-wrapped hulk of the volcano in the middle
of the island. It was an active volcano called Gunungan.
It hadn't erupted for years, but the experts were expect-
ing it to go up any time.

The gang snored in the hold, and Fligh lectured me on
the necessity to free the islands of the world from imperi-

alist domination. I got the impression that he didn't particularly believe a word he was saying. Anyway, as soon as he was sure that the rest of the gang was asleep, he stopped talking.

"Another half hour and we'll be there, Java Jack," he said.

I didn't ask where "there" was. I just kept steady at the controls and tried to avoid looking at the moisture-stained photograph.

Later I learned that we were about a hundred miles away from Tolitoli on the tail end of the wishbone of Sulawesi when Fligh told me to start the descent. We made a smooth landing on an island that wasn't much more than a rock with a lot of scrub, sand, and a couple of palm thickets and three or four other beat-up old planes.

The island was called Freedom Island. It was the hide-out and headquarters of the Free Island Movement. There were a lot of kids there. Nobody all the way grown up. Fligh told me that we were under military discipline, and at war, so anybody who broke the rules would be court-martialed and shot. I kept it in mind.

The kids were a mixed-up bunch. Nobody looked very healthy, and nobody made sense, although there was constant talking going on. The food was lousy, and there wasn't enough of it. We were never allowed to get more than four or five hours of sleep at night. But there was plenty of talk. There were classes in revolutionary tactics, revolutionary rap sessions, and self-criticism periods, at which people would get up and confess to all sorts of crazy things. There was also supposed to be a lot of sex going on—everybody sleeping with everybody—but I never saw any. I think they were all too tired and hungry for that sort of thing.

There really wasn't much work done, and except for ten or fifteen minutes of halfhearted exercise in the morning, all we did was talk and sing revolutionary songs all day. None of this stuff made any sense at all, but I just went along with it. I remembered what Fligh had told me about getting shot.

There were all colors and types and sizes of kids on Freedom Island. There were a couple of Chinese kids, two dropouts from the Japanese Red Army, who were the only ones who really seemed to be having a good time, there were some Albanian refugees, and a sprinkling of long-haired kids from Indonesia, Cambodia, and New Guinea.

The only other American was a black kid from Detroit. His name was Halmahera Harry, and I was never able to say it right, so he sulked. I don't know who made up that name thing—I guess it was Fligh. It was aggravating. You always had to call people by both names, like Sulawesi Sue—otherwise they got insulted and wouldn't talk to you.

One good thing—well, it wasn't really good, just less bad—was that I got to sleep in the best hut on the place, the one with a whole roof. That was because I was a pilot. There were four other pilots. It turned out that none of them knew one-tenth as much about flying as I did. None of them could have handled the big B–17.

One of the things I was supposed to do on the island was instruct the other pilots. We all had the title of Captain. Captain Java Jack. I never did any instructing because the political study schedule never permitted any time, and after a hard day of talking, all the other guys wanted to do was lie around the hut and smoke the local dope and listen to their bellies make noise.

To tell the truth, I lost track of time on Freedom Island. I was there more than a week, maybe more than two, maybe a month. I was just so tired and hungry all the time, and so *bored.* In the beginning, I thought about maybe stealing the B–17 and escaping, but it was guarded, I was guarded, and I couldn't have done it alone. I guess there were probably other kids who wanted out, but I was scared to talk to anybody about it. One of the main activities at the self-criticism sessions was confessing to things other people had done or were planning to do. I was always scared that I would have to see an execution, and even more scared that it would be mine.

Before long, I was looking and talking just like everybody else. I could talk the revolutionary double-talk—if anything was wrong, you blamed it on "the system" and "the imperialists." I still don't know what an imperialist is. I don't think the other kids there knew either. I think Fligh, who was very clearly the boss of the outfit, knew, but didn't really care. All I know about those poor F.I.M. kids is that they were all very, very angry at someone or something, and they were willing to wait around and live badly just so they would finally get a chance to do some damage—and it didn't matter very much who or what was damaged. That's what Fligh was always promising them, that their "sacrifices" would all be worthwhile when they "struck their blow." It was an unhealthy place.

Finally Fligh announced a mission. There was big excitement until it came out that he and I were the only ones going on it. Then things settled down to the usual fantasy land somewhat. Still, there was work to do. The kids were set to work making homemade bombs and decorating the Cessna that Fligh had decided we were going to use. They got busy doodling all sorts of batik designs and cartoons and slogans, and scenes from the Javanese epic war stories. There was a white monkey warrior, and a bunch of damsels in distress, and ogres and giants and all sorts of stuff. It was sloppy work. But I was glad to see Suryo and Charma taking part in it. Apparently they'd been kept in another part of the island, and had decided to sign up rather than get killed. As full-fledged adults, they had a kind of semi-prisoner status, and I thought I'd better not be seen talking to them. I did give them a wink, though.

6   BEFORE DAWN, FLIGH came into the pilots' hut and shook me awake. I followed him to the Cessna with the comic-book paint job. Fligh clambered into the plane first. When I got into the cockpit, I found him hanging something from the compass.

"This is for good luck," he said.

The thing he'd hung on a string from the compass was a spade-shaped piece of leather that had pinholes all over it.

"That's a Gunungan, Java Jack," he explained. "A Gunungan is a figure from the wayang puppet shadow plays. It appears before a war takes place."

Fligh looked into my eyes, which was a scary experience for me. "Let us fight for the liberation of Gunungan Heaven," he said. "For freedom. For your mother and father."

We took off. I had no idea where we were going. There was a machine gun on board, and a bunch of homemade bombs. I was scared. I was scared all the time on Freedom Island, and tired and hungry.

We headed in the direction of Maggasang. It was still dark. Fligh didn't say anything. I was half asleep at the controls. Fligh was in the rear, setting up the machine gun. One of the things I'd always liked about flying was that once you were under way, an airplane was a very good place to think. I had done some of my best thinking while flying, but I wasn't thinking during this flight. I hadn't been thinking very much since arriving at the island; nobody there did a whole lot of thinking, except Fligh.

Suddenly, the whole cockpit filled up with a bright, golden-colored light, and my ears were filled with a hissing noise like a thousand fire extinguishers going at once.

At first, I thought that the bombs had gone off, and that I was having the unique experience of being blown to bits. Or maybe the plane had suddenly caught fire. But it wasn't either of those things.

It was a comet streaking across the sky. It looked close enough to touch, although it was probably thousands of miles away. It was as though you'd waked up to find that the sun had moved into your bedroom. All this was happening in the predawn darkness, and the moon had still been plainly visible. Now the comet crossed straight in front of the moon, making it disappear, and then, as the comet passed, the moon reappeared, sliced in half by the comet's long tail. Then the moon's corona, that ring of light you sometimes see, flared up in rainbow colors. I never saw anything like it.

"So, it's true," Fligh said.

"What?" I asked. "What's true?"

Fligh didn't answer. He just watched the comet, which was now almost out of sight. The golden light disappeared, the cut-in-half moon came back together, and the flaming rings of color around the moon faded away.

"We haven't got much time left," Fligh said. Then he hunched up in his seat and said nothing.

 7 THE NEXT THING Fligh said to me was this: "Java Jack, I just want to remind you about revolutionary discipline. If you don't do what I say when we get there, or if you turn chicken, I'm going to shoot you dead without warning."

"Then we'll both crash," I said.

"You think that worries me?"

I believed it didn't.

We were flying in and out of dark masses of rain clouds that were clumped along Maggasang's mountain ridge and east coast. Mostly we were in the clouds, and I prayed that we wouldn't smash into the cone of Mount Gunungan. We couldn't see a thing, and I had a feeling that the instruments might not be too trustworthy.

I was still shaken by the comet, and the picture of what we'd seen kept coming back to me. It reminded me of the night Charlie and I had flown into Noel, and the story of the Invisible Hunter with his bow and arrow of gold. That night seemed a long time ago.

The Cessna rattled and hummed and whined. One of the side windows wouldn't close all the way, and a stream of cold wet hit me in the neck. I heard some thunder-claps, and there was some kind of a growl going on. I thought it might be the volcano. Maybe the spirit of old Gunungan was snoring.

The sun rose so fast that for an instant I thought the comet was back. The light reflected off the tops of the clouds, and everything was bright. I could see the cap of Gunungan poking up through the clouds. Up near the very top, on the crater ridge, there were tiny fir trees. The base of the volcano was carpeted with thick soupy clouds.

The little spade-shaped Gunungan shadow-play pup-pet Fligh had hung from the compass danced on its string in front of me. The pinholes in the bouncing figure let the brightness through, and sparkled like tiny stars. I could make out pictures, patterns of pinholes: stairs, animals, a gate, a tree. And I could read the words "Fight for the Liberation of the Island of Gunungan Heaven" pricked into the base of the figure.

A big hole in the carpet of clouds floated up to us. It just opened up and we were sailing in clear sky. The island below us looked like a garden, and we must have looked like a crazy-colored butterfly in the comic-book Cessna.

Ribbony rivers turned mirror bright where the sunlight hit them, and the rain forest on the slopes of the mountain looked like black and green fur of some huge animal. Fligh motioned, and I jammed the Cessna down through the hole in the clouds. I could see grasslands beyond the forest line on the mountainside. Rain clouds closed overhead and threw rolling shadows on the landscape. I could see our butterfly shadow flitting along the ground. The plane lurched and the controls jerked out of my hands as we hit a sudden current of air.

"Watch it!" Fligh cried from the rear of the cabin. "You're knocking my stuff around!" A couple of seconds later he was right behind me, digging his fingers into my shoulders. It made me cringe.

"Over there! Look over there, Java Jack!" Fligh shouted. "Yes, those huts. See those long huts between the forest and the grass? Yes—there! That's our hit!" He gloated.

The huts were big, noble-looking buildings with upswept roofs. "What's in the huts, Fligh?" I asked. I didn't get an answer—just a dig in the shoulder and the acciden-tal stroke of an ice-cold pistol along my right temple.

I did what he wanted. I brought us in low across the top of the rain forest, heading toward the grasslands.

Just as our shadow jumped onto the waving grasses, a bunch of naked brown men rushed out of the forest into the grass. They were carrying spears, and kids, and there were women among them. It was obvious that the brightly colored plane didn't suggest anything un-friendly to them.

"Crazies!" Fligh growled. "Those are the crazies who killed your mother and father, Java Jack!"

The Cessna careened toward the mountain. Fligh flipped one of his bombs out the side window. A gust of wind caught us and whipped the dinky plane sideways.

"Stupid Dyaks!" Fligh muttered. The bomb exploded midway between the running Dyaks and the huts. "Bring her back! Bring her back!" Fligh shouted. I was shaking. I couldn't move. He hit me on the back of the head with his fist. "Do it!" he screamed. I pulled up short and swung the Cessna around.

Fligh was hanging out the window firing the machine gun now. I couldn't see what he was shooting at at first. Then I saw the Dyaks diving—or falling—into the grass. I felt dizzy and sick.

"Up, up, up!" Fligh was screaming again.

I was staring at my hands. I couldn't make them do anything. We were about to crash, and I was frozen with fear and sickness. Fligh was screaming and shooting.

Somehow I must have turned the plane around. I don't

remember everything that happened. We made another pass. The thought came to me that Fligh wasn't likely to hit anything, the way I was handling the plane. He must have had the same thought, because he spun around and put a couple of bullets through the wind screen—I felt them whiz past my ear. "Pay attention!" he shouted.

On the next pass I saw one tall native guy racing toward the huts. When we passed over him, he stopped running, stood still, and just looked at us. I could see his face plainly. It was painted like a Pawnee Indian's. He had feathers in his hair. Fligh was going full blast with the gun, but the guy just stood there.

"Magic! It's magic!" Fligh yelled. "Dyak magic!" He was banging on the side of the plane with the gun barrel. "The bullets bounce off him like raindrops!" Fligh cried. "Turn! Turn and go back again!"

We flew over the huts. Khaki-uniformed soldiers started pouring out of the first hut. They were shooting rifles at us. Fligh was shooting and screaming and making weird noises. He threw out two more of the homemade bombs. The first one set the end of one of the huts ablaze. The second made a direct hit in the middle of another. The hut went up like it had twenty tons of dynamite inside—which, in fact, it had, more or less.

"That was it!" Fligh cried. "The sultan's ammo dump!"

Apparently that was what Fligh had come for. Shooting at the Dyaks was just his way of having fun. I headed for a storm cloud. I don't know if Fligh told me it was all right to break away from the fight or not—I didn't care. I didn't care if he shot me. I was getting out of there.

Fligh was all happy and pleased with himself. He was sort of chuckling and patting me on the shoulders. I wanted to throw up. I wondered if we'd managed to kill anybody. It was pretty confusing. With all that shooting, and the bombs, Fligh was almost sure to have killed some people.

It was raining inside the cloud bank. It was thundering too, and a flash of lightning lit up the inside of the cloud. It was a long, lazy whip of lightning that reached down in slow motion. I could hear it crackle as it nicked our right wing.

I felt as though my hands and feet had been hit with a baseball bat. Then I couldn't feel anything.

Fligh was screaming directly into my ear, "Java Jack! Java Jack!" It sounded as though he was calling from the end of a long tunnel. I could see his smooth face receding, getting smaller and smaller and farther away. He tried to pry my hands off the steering. He couldn't do it. I was frozen to the controls. I couldn't move a muscle. Out of the corner of my eye, I saw him strap on the one and only parachute, kick open the door, and bail out. Way down at the end of my tunnel of vision I saw this.

The Cessna burst out into the sunshine again. The little plane was swerving crazily. I caught a glimpse of Fligh's orange parachute popping open like a big flower and slanting away toward the jungles and rivers.

The Cessna came to the end of the steady climb I'd been locked into, lurched—stopped dead in midair—and

then began a slow spiral downward. I was still frozen at
the controls, but I saw everything. The rain was driving
hard now, and the lightning was flashing left and right.
I shot down through the clouds again and the last hole
of sunlight closed up.

There was a crunching, tearing, thumping noise as the
little plane hit the treetops. Very fast, as it descended, the
branches tore the plane to bits, until there was nothing
left but me, somersaulting into the banyan roots by the
river's edge and thudding, face first, into the muddy
water.

 **8** WAY DOWN AT the end of my con-
sciousness I saw a little old lady hover-
ing over me. She had a muddy sarong
tied around her.

I was paralyzed—I didn't know if I
was dead or alive. For all I knew, I'd "crossed over," as
Aunt Amy liked to say, and was already "on the other
side."

"Munah, it is he!" the old lady said to somebody. I
couldn't turn my head or even extend my tunnel vision
to include more than the old lady. "I told you he would
come!" she said, and started to cry.

The hole in the black cloud I was looking through
enlarged a little, and I saw a young girl—maybe fourteen, maybe older, I couldn't tell. She was holding my
ankles up in the air. "Yes, Ibu, you told me," she said.

The old lady was bending over me and poking at me. I could only half feel her old fingers in a far-off way; it was as if somebody were touching me through layers of blankets. "Bring him in, daughter—" she was thumping on my breastbone now—"it's raining too hard to examine him properly out here."

The old lady picked me up under the arms, and the two of them carried me through a doorway. I was able to see a little better, and I could see that they had brought me into a sort of half cave, half hut. The hut part was sort of poked into a hillside, and the cave part was just a scooped-out place in the dirt. There was another, smaller doorway at the far side of the cave-hut, leading into the hill—a tunnel.

There was an oil lamp burning in the hut. Beside it was a frame made of teak. I knew what it was; I had one like it back in Neosho. My parents had sent it. It was a thing to hang batiks on. A long piece of silky white material was hanging from the frame. A brass batik-wax melter was smoking near my head. Next to it was a box of wax-pens. Next to the box was a squat stone vat. I knew what all this stuff was for from reading articles about Java, and from all the stuff my folks had written and sent to me.

Batik is a way of dyeing paintings into cloth. First wax is painted on while it's hot, and then the colors go on. Wherever there is wax, no color can go, so that part stays white, or whatever color went on last. The finished cloth looks like nothing in the world except batik.

The old lady's way of dealing with sick or hurt people appeared to be thumping, poking, slapping, and pinching. She worked all over my body with quick light movements. At first she had obviously been poking me to see what might be broken, but now she was working all over me as though I was a piano and she was a piano player. She was kneading me like a bunch of dough that she was making a person out of.

"Now he'll be all right," she said. "Munah, you can clean him up—I have to finish my work."

In fact, I did feel as though I'd be all right. Before the old lady had gone to work poking and plucking and twanging on my body, I suddenly realized, I had been dying. Now I felt strangely—it's hard to express this—lined up. As if a checkerboard had been set up for a game, and then somebody had bumped the table, and then all the pieces, which had been all everywhere, had been set back in their proper squares.

Munah, the young girl, went to work washing my face and cleaning some big scratches and bruises with oil from a bottle.

Ibu took the oil lamp and moved into the tunnel opening at the back of the hut. She set the lamp down just inside the tunnel entrance. The flickery light was caught up by veins of silvery gray and goldish copper-colored metal. The old woman was poking around in soggy baskets, moving tools, hand picks, out of the way, looking for something. She found it. She picked it up. I couldn't see what it was. She wiped it on her dirty sarong. "Just a few more hours," she said.

"I cannot work now," Ibu mumbled, "it is too dark. The final finish has to be perfect. The rain must stop."

She looked at the leaky ceiling. "Stop!" she commanded. It went on raining. "I have promised the sultan," she murmured to herself over and over.

"Ibu, the sultan does not need it yet," Munah said. "Why do you worry so?"

The old woman frowned at me. I still couldn't move an eyelash, and I was starting to hurt all over, as if I'd been burned.

"If we are late," Ibu said, "if I should fail . . ."

"Then the sultan might refuse to marry me?" Munah asked.

The old lady nodded. She hobbled over to me and looked down into my face. She looked to be floating eight or ten feet above me.

"You are the answer to my prayers, young man—do you know that?"

I couldn't say yes and I couldn't say no.

"After the sign in the sky last night, I prayed. I prayed for you to come to me." She shook her finger at me. "And you have come! You have come to perform the mission!" she cried. I'd already performed one "mission" for Fligh and wondered what sort Ibu had in mind. She sank to her knees and her old gray head wobbled as she put her ear to my chest.

"Maybe he is dead," Munah said softly. "He doesn't move. His heart doesn't beat."

"No, he is not dead," Ibu said. "He is suspended between life and death. We will call him back. Munah, what is his name? Find his name!"

Munah fished around in my pockets. Fligh had taken

my passport and my traveler's check, but I was wearing my F.I.M. medallion. Munah fished the cutout brass map of Java from inside my torn shirt. "Look," she said to Ibu, "Java. Jack. Java Jack."

"Java Jack," the old lady said sternly, "wake up. You are not dead. I know it. You are the answer to my prayer. The answer to my prayer is not dead."

I didn't quite follow Ibu's logic in this, but I did want to find out if what she said was true. I told myself it was all or nothing. A maximum effort. I pushed everything I had into the little finger of my left hand.

"Look, Ibu, look!" Munah said. "His finger. It moves. He's alive!"

That was a relief.

The old woman was satisfied. She looked at me for a while. My eyelids started to work. As soon as they began to work they felt heavy. I was exhausted. The shock of the crash and everything that had gone before it—the news of my parents' death, the long trip, the weird experiences with Fligh and the F.I.M., the comet during the flight, the shooting and bombing, the lightning—it all began to wear off, and hurt.

"He's crying, Ibu," Munah said.

"Good," Ibu said, "it's the surest sign of life. Now you must make him a map. Use Father's book. Copy the map from the book. Show the Water Palace, the bay, the river. . . ." Ibu paused and thought about something while she stared at me. "But he won't understand Maggasang writing, will he? The picture is all written in Maggasang language, so you must write the names in English—the sea, the island, the town—make it all in English."

"Yes, Ibu," Munah answered. She rummaged around in a trunk and dragged out an old tattered book. She smoothed it open and set it on a rack near the piece of white silk. She dipped her fingers into the box of wax-pens, pulled one out, heated it up, blew on it, and started to hum.

When the wax was molten hot she picked up the pen, and her fingers began to fly with it over the piece of silk. It was amazing. Squiggles and curlicues and shapes flew from the pen like magic.

Just as I was about to drop off to sleep, and could feel my breathing for the first time, the ground started shaking.

Munah stopped working. She looked at the ceiling— to see if it was about to fall in, I guess. The earthquake didn't seem to bother her. I guessed she was used to earthquakes. I wasn't, but I fell asleep anyway.

When I woke up, the hut was filled with little brown and black kids. They were all watching Munah. She was taking a piece of dark, wet cloth out of the stone vat. After wringing it, she shook it out. There was a pinkish yellow light coming into the hut. It made the wet batik shine with colors like a peacock's tail.

"That's beautiful," I heard myself say. My voice sounded hoarse and strange.

The kids all jumped when I spoke. "Where did they come from?" I asked.

"They're Dyak children, Java Jack," Munah answered.

"Don't Dyaks . . . uh . . . hunt heads?" I was remembering things Fligh had said.

"They used to, Java Jack, but not anymore." Munah had a fat black iron stuffed with burning coals. She was ironing the batik. The steam from the iron puffed around the room, and the wet batik hissed where the iron touched it. When Munah held it up again, it was more beautiful than it had been before. The colors were like stained glass.

"What's that rainbow doing there?" I asked.

"That's part of the flag of the island of Equator," Munah said. "It's from the old Dyak legend about the beginning of the world."

It reminded me of the comet I'd seen in the plane with Fligh, the rainbowlike bands around the moon when it had been cut in half by the comet's golden tail.

Munah must have guessed what I was thinking. "You saw it too? In the sky?"

"Yes, I saw it. The comet."

"We don't know what it was," Munah said, "but we know it was the sign of the Qris."

"Kris?" I said with a frown. "You mean one of those daggers with the wavy blade?"

Munah smiled. "Qris is not kris with a 'k'—it is Qris with a 'Q.' Long ago there was no kris, only Qris."

"What's Qris with a 'Q'?"

"It's what you saw in the sky."

We were starting to go in circles. "What does it mean?"

"It means the material—" Munah stopped and put her hands over her mouth. It was all quiet. The Dyak kids had left. All I could hear were a few birds and the sound of "clink, clink, clink" coming from somewhere.

Munah started again, blushing—she had obviously begun to tell me something she wasn't supposed to. Now she was going to try to draw my attention away from what she had started to say. She did it too.

"It means a story," she said. "Once the world had two lands, and both were round. People then were tall like giants. They were able to know, before it happened, that a fearsome event would strike the Earth. They fled to a fiery star. Before they went, they hid a treasure for the new men on Earth—the ones who would come later. This treasure they hid in a cavern in a place the fearsome event would not destroy. That place became the island of Equator. To guard the treasure, they left one of their people behind.

"The fearsome event changed the Earth. What was East and West became North and South. Where there had been water, land appeared. The guardian of the treasure was not touched by these changes in the Earth because he lived on the island of Equator, which the first people, the giants, knew would be protected against the fearsome event.

"The guardian of the treasure lived and hunted with a magical bow and arrow. The new men on Earth, the little men, who reached the shores of the island of Equator could not see him—but they could hear his canoe, and see his footprints, and hear his voice."

"This is the same as a Pawnee Indian story about the Invisible Hunter!" I said. "I heard it long ago at home!"

Munah smiled patiently. "A lot of old stories are the same, Java Jack. This one is also like 'Cinderella.' "

I must say it's weird, listening to a local fairy tale in a jungle halfway around the world when it's the same one you used to hear in Neosho, Missouri.

"The Invisible Hunter," Munah went on, "told the new people of the island of Equator that he would marry the girl who could really see what he looked like."

"Yes!" I was getting caught up in the whole thing now. "That's the way it goes! And all the girls in the village went down to the water at sunset, and they'd hear his canoe coming, and strain their eyes trying to see him, but they couldn't. Instead of being honest, they'd make up all sorts of things and pretend they had seen them. Finally, the hunter said that the girl who could describe his bow and arrow would be the one he'd marry. The others tried to lie again, but only the Ash Girl was able to describe it—"

Munah interrupted:

> "His bow is the bow of the rainy day,
> His strap is the moon growing old.
> His bow is strung with the Milky Way,
> His arrow a comet of gold."

All of a sudden I felt something very tender for Munah —because she'd said a poem to me, and because she was beautiful, and homely like the Ash Girl, and maybe nobody would ever notice that she was beautiful. Maybe nobody would ever see her bathed in the light of her rainbow batik and hear her say a poem. So I felt all this love for her—and said something stupid, which is typical of me with girls.

"Don't worry, Munah," I said. "You'll marry the sultan."

She turned red, and then spun around so I wouldn't see her crying. It was quiet. I heard the "clink, clink, clink" noise again. Munah was sort of hugging herself, keeping her back to me. I knew that anything I might say would make it worse, that I should just keep my mouth shut and let this uncomfortable moment blow over. Of course, I didn't listen to myself, and tried saying I was sorry, or something like that, which made the embarrassment worse. Munah just waved her hand back and forth, as if to say, "Never mind."

I shut up for a while and let things cool off. I didn't really understand exactly how I'd managed to make us both feel so embarrassed, but I'd done it, all right.

After a while, I thought I might try to start some conversation. "Uh, Munah . . . where's Ibu? I was thinking I ought to talk to her . . . to thank her for helping me. . . . And I want to thank you too."

The clouds had lifted. Munah was back to normal. She smiled at me.

"If there's anything I can do for Ibu and you . . ." I went on.

"Java Jack, you do not have to do something for Ibu unless you want to truly. While you slept this morning, you were dreaming. In your dream you said 'Mother!

Mother!' and 'Father! Father!' many times. You are looking for them, aren't you?"

I felt a little silly about talking in my sleep. "Yes."

"You should look for them first. Who are they?"

I told Munah my whole story. As I talked, I sipped a
sort of light soup she brought me. I was feeling better
every minute, although I was sore in all the places Ibu
had poked and pinched. When I had finished telling
Munah everything, she smiled at me.

"Ibu is right after all," she said. "You should take
something to the Sultan of Equator."

"What made you change your mind? Before you said
that I ought to look for my mother and father first. Does
knowing who they were . . . are . . . does that make a
difference? Munah, do you know something about my
parents? Do you know that they are dead?"

Somehow, even as I asked the question, I knew what
Munah would answer. She was too sweet to smile like
that if she knew my parents were dead.

"They are alive, Java Jack," she said. "They are alive
in Equator." She pointed at the map. It showed a round
island, and her long finger touched a drawing of a palace.
"They live in the Water Palace on the island of Equator."

"So," I said.

"So," Munah said, giggling, "if Java Jack does something for Ibu, it's on the way he has to go anyway."

I was hardly surprised to find that I could stand up and
walk, if a little stiffly. Munah handed me the map, and I
went out to find Ibu.

 **9** CLINK, CLINK, CLINK.

The sound came from a clearing not far from the hut. I could see the river, and a hunk of the Cessna sticking into the muddy bank.

Rain forest rose on all sides of the clearing. The light was clean and clear after the rain of the night before, and the trees and big-leaved plants gleamed wet and dark. There was a mist rising from the forest.

Clink, clink, clink.

Some Dyak kids were clustered around a big stone in the middle of the clearing. Ibu, wrapped in a woven shawl, knelt by the stone, pounding away with an iron hammer. Metal on stone. Clink, clink, clink. Three clinks. Pause. Three clinks again. Pause. It went like that.

Ibu looked up. She didn't seem to notice what was hanging over her head. I don't know how she could have missed it. It seemed to be growing right there like one of the forest plants. It rose up straight for maybe fifty feet, and then began curving away, arching over the clouds. It was a rainbow! Every color was as clear as a crayon in your hand, and every band as wide as a bed sheet.

I was amazed, seeing a rainbow that close up. There wasn't any pot of gold, just an old Maggasang lady and a bunch of headhunter kids. It seemed as though a rainbow practically on top of their heads was nothing special to them. The thing that really impressed me was how solid it was. I mean, it had *thickness!* You could put your arms around it. At home, rainbows were always far-off and airy. This looked as if you could take a saw and cut off a slice. It made me think of cartoons in which people walk on a rainbow like a bridge. It also made me think of Munah's poem and the Invisible Hunter. "His bow is the bow of the rainy day, his strap is the moon growing old." Some bow. Some giant.

Something flashed in my eye. I thought for a moment that sombody was flashing a mirror, but it was something in Ibu's hand. She was holding it up and looking at it, and every now and then it flashed brilliantly.

When I came close, the Dyak kids scattered. Ibu had quit her hammering and started grinding. Sometimes she made the sound you get by scraping your fingernails on a blackboard or an ice pick on glass. Screech, screech, crunch. I winced. I looked over her shoulder. She was grinding what looked like a needle. It was gold, but brighter than any gold I had ever seen.

"You're all well now, Java Jack," she said.

"Yes." I *was* all well. In fact, I felt pretty good, if a little beaten up.

"You were mostly dead last night," she said.

"I know."

"It took a lot of doing, but I got you all lined up again," Ibu said. She apparently looked at what she'd been doing with all the poking and thumping in the same way I had imagined it.

"Thank you, Ibu," I said.

"Do you have the map?"

"Yes. Munah gave it to me."

"Good. I will finish the needle in a short time. Then you can take it to the sultan. He is waiting for it."

Screech, screech, crunch.

"If you succeed in delivering it, I will cancel the debt you owe to me and Munah."

"Debt?" I asked stupidly.

"Yes. We saved your life. Besides, you came in an airplane, and did much harm to many of our people."

I had been afraid Ibu and Munah would hear about the raid with Fligh. I had no idea how far we were from the place where Fligh had done all the shooting. I thought the word would get around, but I didn't know how fast. I tried to explain. "Ibu, I was in the airplane, I even flew it—but I was forced to go along. I didn't know . . . I mean, I wasn't . . . and I'm truly grateful for being dragged out of the river, and I know you saved my life. . . ."

"Words, Java Jack, words. You must show me," Ibu said.

Screech, screech, crunch.

10 TEN HOURS AFTER I had said good-bye to Ibu and Munah, I was standing on top of a hill looking down toward the town of Maggasang, beside the sea. The moon rose, sort of squashed and yellow, behind the clumps of clouds on the horizon. The rest of the sky was clear and starry, except for a trail of smoke from the crater of Mount Gunungan that made a dark swath across the sky.

The town didn't look like much more than a single street with huts and houses bunched up on either side, and a scooped-out harbor with a bunch of Bugis prahus at anchor. Out in the middle of the harbor lay the dark hulk of a ship, a freighter of some kind, with a dull red lamp glowing on the stern.

I looked down at the map Munah had made. The batik drawings shimmered strangely in the moonlight. I was approaching the town where I ought to be able to find a boat to take me to this island of Equator. I looked at the island on the map. It wasn't a real map-type map with a scale of miles, so I had no idea how far away the island was, or how big it was—or even if its position on the map had anything to do with where it really was.

Ibu and Munah had given me a wad of money. Probably it didn't amount to more than a couple of dollars. Still, way out in the islands you never know how much a couple of bucks will buy. Maybe it would be enough to hire a boat to go to Equator.

I was getting hungry. The rice patties Munah had given me were supposed to last for a day and a half, maybe two days, but I had eaten the last of them hours ago. I was still hungry. I should have explained to them that I had been half starved by the F.I.M. folks for weeks before this.

The repair job Munah had done on my clothes was holding up well enough. Ibu's repair job on my body was good too—good enough for me to have waded across a river and picked my way on very rough trails for a whole day.

I started down the hill toward the town. I still had some dense forest to go through on the way down the slope. I was a little nervous about meeting a tiger. I knew there were still plenty of them in Maggasang. My fingers found the needle, which was hanging around my neck along with my brass Java Jack emblem. Ibu had strung it so that the brass map of Java covered the needle. "You never know who you will meet, Java Jack," she had warned me. "There are men who would kill to get this needle." And tigers too.

Java Jack. The name was sticking. Even I was starting to call myself Java Jack. Munah had worked it into the batik, with the inscription "To Java Jack the Pirate" across the top of the thing. I had hated the name all along —at least when the F.I.M. people had used it, and Fligh. I think I started liking it when Munah continued to call me that even after she knew my real name.

It was spooky going through the forest at night. It would be completely dark, as dark as the inside of a closet, and then suddenly there would be a shaft of moonlight bright enough to read by, and everything around would be bright for a yard or so—and then blackness again.

I crashed out of the thick forest into the backyard of a big old house. It was a mansion, in fact, and pretty old. It was built like some old houses I had seen in Jakarta, going from the airport on the way to Surabaya. It might have been a couple of centuries old. It had columns, and a dome with an iron weather vane. It looked a little like the courthouse in Joplin, Missouri. And it was completely deserted.

You can tell when there's nobody in a house—when it's empty, and not just asleep. There wasn't any doubt in my mind that there wasn't a person, dog, or cat in that house. I wondered if there was any food.

There was a back verandah on the house. There was an outdoor kitchen too. From somewhere, maybe from when I was a little tiny kid in Java, I remembered that the old Dutch-style houses had these outdoor kitchens, so the cooking wouldn't heat up the house in warm weather.

Everything was in place in the kitchen—big black pots and ladles—everything but food. Nobody had cooked there for a long time. The low stone ovens were neatly swept out. I couldn't even smell food. This disappointed me. I was seriously hungry.

Then it occurred to me that maybe there was an indoor kitchen too. Breaking into houses was never something I had an interest in doing—but eating was. I had a little fight with my conscience while I stood there in the out-door kitchen. It was odd, in a way. I had taken part in a raid and, for all I knew, helped to murder innocent peo-ple, and here I was debating with myself about breaking into a house and stealing a little food. Of course, this was different—I was on my own, and in the plane I'd had no choice. Anyway, hunger won the argument, and I set about breaking into the house.

The windows were rather high off the ground, but not hard to open. I found one that hinged inward, and was able to force it by simply pushing with a long stick I'd picked up. Now all I had to do was scramble up the side of the house, a matter of five feet, and haul myself through.

I was in the middle of doing this, of hauling myself through, when a very strong hand grabbed a handful of Java Jack and did the hauling for me.

11 WHAT DO YOU say to someone who helps you break into a house—from the inside? I said, "Thanks."

"Okay, kid, okay," boomed a voice.

I still couldn't see who was talking, even though he was holding me by the front of my shirt, and my feet were dangling above the floor.

It was somebody big, that much I could tell, even before he swung me around into a patch of moonlight and put me down.

"Don't worry, kid. Nobody home," the big guy said. I *was* worried. It seemed to me that I had run into a burglar, a housebreaker—although that's what I was too. The big guy was about six feet tall. He had gotten hold of my Java medallion and was studying it in the moonlight. This gave me a chance to have a look at him. His shoulders were like the bumps on a water buffalo's back. His chest was thick too. His face was broad and friendly. He had a row of bright uneven teeth, thick lips, and a neat black mustache that curled up at the ends. His eyebrows curved up in a quizzical way, and underneath them his eyes shone out like big black coins. He was the sort of person you can't help liking, even when you're scared of him—which I was.

He was still studying my medallion. The needle had fallen inside my shirt. I was glad of that, remembering Ibu's warning about people wanting to steal it.

"I can read," he said, "listen. J-A-V-A. Hah! Hear that? J-A-C-K." He laughed a big belly laugh that filled up the room.

"Don't worry about noise, kid. Like I say, nobody home. Just you and me." He went back to his reading, "Java. Jack. Java. Jack."

This was getting on my nerves. I waited while he put it all together.

"Ooohooo! I got it! *You!* You Java Jack! Right? Java Jack, how do you do?" He stuck out his hand for me to shake. It was as big as a shovel.

"How do you do?" he repeated. "You Java Jack," he announced to the yard and the forest behind us. Then he waved at the moon. "And me? I am Bunga! Bunga the Bugis!"

He took my hand again. It was still numb from the first time he'd shaken it. "You know what is Bunga?"

"I'm sorry—no, I don't."

"Bunga means flower in Malay language. Blossom. Bugis, my people." He laughed. "I am Blossom the Bugis." Then he smiled the biggest smile I'd ever seen. "But my famous name not Blossom, not Bugis. My famous name is what? You know?"

He had on one of those brimless Muslim hats, like the ones I'd seen the men wearing in the Surabaya airport, but his wasn't black. It was lamb's fur and trimmed in scarlet and gold batik. He had on a shiny satin shirt that was red too, and it had batik pictures of kris knives and peacocks and Lord-knows-what all over it. His trousers were green batiked cotton, and his legs stuck out of the frayed edges like a pair of teak table legs—the kind carved with lion's feet and claws. He was barefoot. His toes splayed out unevenly, like his teeth. His feet looked as if they were glued to the ground wherever he put them.

"What my famous name? What?"

I sensed that it was worth any risk if I could guess this guy's, this Bunga the Bugis', famous name. I knew the Bugis were famous as pirates from way back—and the rest I could pretty much guess.

"I know," I said. "You are the Batik Pirate."

Bunga the Bugis grabbed me and started squeezing the life out of me. Now I knew what it felt like to be eaten by a python. "You know! You know!" he crowed. "You know me! I *am* the Batik Pirate!"

He was like a little kid. Tears popped out of his eyes from happiness. You'd think that nobody had ever recognized him or heard his famous name before. Not true. I later found out that Bunga the Bugis was a widely respected and feared professional pirate. Up until that moment, I was probably the only person for hundreds and hundreds of miles around who *didn't* know who he was. But that didn't make him any less delighted that I knew his name. What accounted for the tears was that Bunga the Bugis, Blossom the Bugis, the Batik Pirate, was the easiest man I ever saw to laugh or cry or shout or dance or get angry. That's just how he was.

12 "COME ON, YOU Java Jack! We go eat."
Bunga the Bugis set me down as if I were a puppet.

"Plenty food here. Bunga cook. You look around. This mighty nice big house —belong to Tuan Robinson."

"Tuan Doctor Jeffrey Robinson?" I asked. My heart was thumping.

"Yah," Bunga grunted. "Blossom welcome you, Java Jack, to house of Tuan Robinson. You hungry?"

"I'm starving," I said, "but what—"

"Good. Bunga make fried rice—special Bugis *nasi goreng*. Okay?"

"Okay, Bunga, but—"

"Oohoo, you like Bugis cooking. Good!"

"But where is Tuan Robinson?" I managed to get the words out.

"Gone."

"Gone where?"

"Nobody knows where. Some people say Dyak took his head, but nobody knows for sure. Not even Batik Pirate knows. Anyway, Tuan Robinson one good man. If he dead, he say, 'Hey you men, better eat my food!'

If he alive, he gonna buy more food soon."

Bunga lit a ruby glass oil lamp. The room flickered with red light and our shadows. "You look around, Java Jack. Some mighty nice big house, this one. I go cook."

I was already looking. I was looking for something to tell me for sure that this had been my parents' house. There was a big map of Maggasang on the wall. I looked closely, trying to find something I recognized. I thought I located the bend in the river where I had come down in the Cessna. It was right up inside a kind of gorge that poked into the side of Mount Gunungan. I found the mansion we were in at the moment, drawn in and labeled "Maggasang Observatory."

If this was an observatory, then probably the dome I'd seen had a telescope inside. I picked up the lamp and went into the next room. Bunga was singing in the indoor kitchen.

On the way, I checked the bookcase. There were three copies of *Dyak Love and Legends,* the book my parents had written. There were a lot of other books, many of them about earthquakes—seismology—books about volcanos, a lot of them. There was one book that was more like the stuff you'd find in my parents' house. It was called *Fairy Tales Around the World.* I opened it up, and strangely enough, a section called "The Invisible Hunter" was marked in pencil.

There was a lot of stuff in the house, the sort of things my parents had sent to me in Neosho, only lots more.

One of the rooms had a high ceiling and an organ. A big one. I love organs. I don't know how to play; I just like to fool with them. I couldn't resist this one. I pulled out some stops, pumped it up, and hit a chord. It made quite a noise.

"Hey! Shut that noise!" Bunga came running in carrying two platters of rice and peppers and fried eggs and tomatoes and carrots and stuff. "You can hear that all the way down on the waterfront, Java Jack, so no noise please. Now eat."

We sat on the organ bench and scooped up the hot food. It was spicy and greasy and good. We mopped the plates with our fingers. After we were finished, Bunga broke a *kretek* in two, offered me half, and struck a match on the sole of a bare foot.

We sat smoking and digesting. I guess a full stomach dampens the high you get from *kreteks,* because I didn't get the same cushion-shoe effect I had had in Jakarta.

"What you doing in Maggasang?" Bunga asked.

I liked this big pirate, but he *was* a pirate, and I had to play it safe. I'd already thought of asking him to help me get to the island of Equator, but I didn't want to let him in on my whole story—not yet, at any rate.

"I came here to meet Dr. Robinson," I said.

"He gone," said Bunga, as if he hadn't already told me.

"Well, I want to find him. I think I know where he is."

"Good. Where?"

"He's on an island."

"Fine. Now which one? Many island around here. You know which one?"

"It's called Equator," I said. "It's got a sultan."

"Most island have sultan. Bunga the Bugis knows most island—never hear of this one, Equator. Maybe it has another name?"

"If it does, I don't know it," I said.

As well as I could remember, there wasn't anything on the map Munah had made for me that revealed who had made it, or why. I figured it would be safe to show it to the Bugis pirate. "I've got a map," I said.

I handed Bunga the batik map. He looked at it. He read the words "To Java Jack the Pirate."

"Oohoo!" Bunga said. "How come you don't tell Blossom you are pirate too?"

"I'm not really," I said. "The person who made this map just thinks I am."

"Oh. She must like you," Bunga the Bugis said. He fingered the silky batik. "Nice. Nice batik. Nice woman make this. She your girl, Java Jack?"

"No," I said.

"Maybe Bunga like to meet who made this nice batik," the Bugis said. "Where you come from, Java Jack the Pirate?" he asked.

"America. Neosho, Missouri."

Bunga thought awhile, and looked at the burning end of his cigarette. "Look. We Bugis say something—'Many questions make few friends.' You understand? Sorry I make questions. Let's just be friends. Okay?" He held out his greasy hand. Our handshake was sticky but sincere.

"Look, Java Jack, maybe I help you, huh? You want to

go to island. I got ship. Maybe I take you, huh?"

"I've got some money," I said. "It isn't much, but
. . ."

Bunga's face clouded over. "Bunga the Bugis never
take money. Got no money." He turned out his pockets.
There were cigarettes and toothpicks, some rope and
some dried hot peppers, but no money. "See? Friends
don't need money."

He clapped me on the back. "I go upstairs. You come
too. Bunga go to toilet. You look in Tuan Robinson's big
telescope. You can see moon. Soon we go to your island
—what name?"

"Equator."

"Yah."

More luck. When I denied being a pirate, Bunga the
Bugis thought I was being modest and high-class. In his
opinion, there was nothing better than being a pirate.
And he knew I was a pirate—it said so on my map. So
now we were friends for sure. We got to the second
floor.

"Toilet here and big telescope up there." Bunga motioned to a narrow staircase that led to a third story. He
knew the house so well that I decided to ask a question.

"Bunga, have you come here often?" I asked. "I mean
as Tuan Robinson's guest?"

"Many questions make few friends," Bunga answered.

I guess I looked embarrassed.

"But I tell you what," he said with his hand on the
bathroom doorknob. "It's like this. Down in Maggasang,

town toilet not very good, you know? And on my ship, worse. I tell you this—sometimes I come here, use toilet. Okay?"

"Okay, Bunga." I laughed.

While Bunga was in the john, I climbed upstairs with the red-shaded oil lamp. There was a fairly big telescope, bigger than I'd expected to find way out here in Maggasang. It was pointed through a slot in the dome. I looked into the eyepiece. It was pointed right at a cluster of stars. I remembered the sign of the Qris. I wondered if Bunga had seen it too. I went downstairs and banged on the toilet door.

"Almost finish," Bunga said through the door.

"Take your time," I said. "I just want to ask you a question."

"What question?"

"Did you see something the other night—in the sky?"

Silence. After a while the door opened. Bunga was buckling his belt as he came out. He left his oil lamp in the bathroom. It was obviously a place to think in. There were rows and rows of paperback books lining the green enamel walls. Bunga had stuffed a book into his belt. I saw the title—*Captain Blood.*

"Practicing your reading?" I asked.

"Yah, Java Jack, I can read, you know?" Bunga yawned. "The other night. Yah, I see lots of things. What thing you mean?" His eyes twinkled as he tried to pretend he didn't know what I was talking about. I crossed my arms on my chest and waited. He shrugged.

"Yah. Big bow and arrow in sky. You mean that, huh,

Java Jack? I see that. Means bad, if you ask Blossom. No good at all. Dyak all think it mean old Gunungan gonna blow up. Bugis think it bad luck, don't know what kind. Bunga don't know what about it. How about you, Java Jack?"

"I don't know either," I said. "If it's all right with you, I'd like to look around some more."

"Okay, but not too long," Bunga the Bugis said. "Bunga will read for a while."

On the stairs, I brushed against a big flip switch on the wall. Before Bunga could say anything, I flipped the thing, just out of curiosity—not thinking. In two seconds a generator somewhere started rumbling. A few seconds later the whole house was blazing with electric light.

"Now we got maybe twenty minutes, and that's all, Java Jack," Bunga said with a grin. "Anybody down in Maggasang town look up and see the lights, they think for sure Tuan Robinson back, and they all gonna come up here to say hello. Might as well leave the lights on—" Bunga spread his hands in a helpless gesture—"everybody seen them already. Go on, look around now."

In the next ten minutes, I went from item to item—looking for something—I didn't know what.

"Pretty soon we gotta go," the Bugis said, "otherwise you put in jail for trespassing. Probably you got no passport, huh?"

There were big charts on the wall. One batch of charts was a series of cross-sections of Mount Gunungan—from the side, from the top, from various angles. The drawings showed a maze of tunnels inside and underneath the mountain. Some of these were marked as lava-flow and lava-release trails. The structure of the mountain fascinated me. It had three cones—the big outer one that everybody sees, and two small inner cones that must have been covered by clouds when Fligh and I flew over. According to the charts, the big crater was about thirty miles in diameter. It made me think of a huge cauldron. A few red lines were marked "probable path of eruption," and in tiny red pencil letters, partially erased, somebody had written "star tunnel."

Then there were charts that were labeled as seismological graphs, with years marked going all the way back to 1888. There was a big painting that showed a circular city in the middle of a wide plain. Underneath the city was a set of tunnels radiating like spokes from a central cave.

Another section of wall was covered with things called Spectrogram Analysis Pictographs—that's what the card mounted on the wall said. I couldn't make head nor tail of them. And there were glass cases with Petri dishes inside, each with different colored crystals in it, and one dish with a yellowish gray blob that seemed to be vibrating or breathing. Next to the blob was a thick typed book, held together with a rubber band. The title was *Organic Properties of Inorganic Substances.*

Bunga was pushing me toward the door. "But, Bunga, why don't we just wait and talk to whoever turns up?" I was half planning to announce that I was Tuan Robinson's son when the people arrived. They couldn't do anything to me for being in my own father's house, after all.

"Don't talk so silly, Java Jack," Bunga said. "Don't you know everybody looking for you Free Island kids? Soon they see you—whop, put you in jail, then forget about you. I fix it so nobody bother you. You come with Bunga. You be real pirate for sure now, Java Jack."

Bunga dumped a box of cassette tapes out onto the floor. He picked one out. It said "Bach—Prelude and Fugue" on the outside. Bunga the Bugis put the cassette into the stereo player.

"People come, hear this," he chortled, "they think Tuan inside playing records as usual—then they think about maybe they should wait until he's through. They spend an hour anyway trying to be polite. Meantime, we gone long time. Now we run, Java Jack."

We ran. Bunga took a forest route he evidently knew by heart. It led away from town and then doubled back. We ran the whole way. Actually, we went at a sort of dogtrot. I had a chance to think as we puffed along the narrow path. Bunga knew about the Freedom Island kids, and he thought I was one of them on the run— which, in fact, I was.

We came out in a dead-end alley that empties into the main street of Maggasang.

As we reached the boardwalk that runs beside the mud boulevard, we saw a crowd of people on the opposite side of the street pointing up at the Maggasang Observatory. The mansion shone brightly with electric lights, and the wind carried snatches of organ music into the town. It was the usual spooky organ music you hear in monster movies.

Bunga tapped in code on the back door of a shop at the corner of the alley and the street.

"Now we fix you up," he told me.

The door opened. A Chinese girl peeked out, looked both ways, and whisked us into the shop.

 13 BUNGA SAUNTERED DOWN the wooden sidewalk with his arm around the Chinese girl. He was talking to her in pidgin Cantonese, the half-baked Chinese dialect that sailors learn in Macao and Hong Kong and Singapore—anywhere in Southeast Asia.

She didn't look like she understood much of what he was saying, but that didn't bother Bunga. He was content just to show off to the lesser mortals who shuffled off the wooden slats and sloshed in the mud to avoid confronting him.

As the two of them made their way toward the Rumah Agung Restaurant and Hotel, people whispered, "Look out, here comes the Batik Pirate." Bunga had changed clothes at the Chinese shop, where he kept a stash of fancy duds. He was wearing a purple silk shirt covered with batik flowers, and black velvet trousers with white and purple batik trim.

The Chinese girl wasn't the same one who had opened the door for us. As a matter of fact, it wasn't even a girl —it was me, Java Jack, with an inch of makeup pasted all over my face, and wearing a long black wig and a fancy Chinese dress that reached to the ground. How Bunga had talked me into this crazy playacting, I was still trying to understand. We must have looked like something out of the gold rush days in San Francisco—I mean the whole scene, the wooden sidewalk, the saloons, the mud street; we were suddenly in the middle of your standard Wild West movie.

The Chinese girl back at the shop had just about died laughing while she and Bunga got me all rigged up in this outfit. I, of course, was dying of embarrassment, but I had found out something about Bunga the Bugis. He always got his way.

The other thing I found out was that we were on our way to see Fligh—yes, the same Fligh I had escaped from. He was still alive—I wasn't surprised to learn that—and was upstairs in the old Rumah Agung.

We made our way through the shabby town. Oil workers staggered around drunk, and gangs of Japanese outboard motor salesmen wandered around trying to have a good time.

We walked into the Rumah Agung. Old Huip, the Dutch proprietor, raised his eyebrows, but he didn't dare say anything, in case Bunga got mad. Bunga and his men were good customers. As far as I was concerned, we weren't fooling anybody. Bunga, of course, was delighted with the whole business, and was sure we were fooling everybody.

"Beer for me, and a Dr. Pepper for Blue Blossom," Bunga said in a big voice. "Huip, meet Blue Blossom.

Blue Blossom, meet Huip."

Huip and I shook hands. I could see that the old man was having a hard time not laughing out loud.

"Shei-shei," I said in what I hoped sounded like a Chinese girl's voice. It was the only Chinese word I knew. Bunga's girl friend in the shop had taught it to me. "You say *shei-shei* any time—okay," she'd said. I think it means thank you.

Bunga was convinced that I was hooked up with the Free Island crazies, and there was no way I could convince him that I had been taken to Freedom Island by force, and was just as happy never to see it again. I was also afraid of Fligh, and said so, but Bunga said, "How Fligh gonna know it's you in neat disguise? Besides, nobody can do anything to any friend of the Batik Pirate —not in this place."

Bunga was pushing me toward the stairs. "Why don't you leave Blue Blossom with me in the back room?" Huip asked. "Fligh is going to see right through this masquerade, so what's the point?" I wondered if anybody in Maggasang *didn't* know what Bunga was up to.

"Gonna pull it off, Huip," Bunga said; and then to me, "Take Dr. Pepper with you. Act dumb. Giggle a lot." And then to Huip again, "Fligh won't look sideways at Blue Blossom."

Bunga grabbed my sweaty arm and pushed me up the stairs. I almost broke my neck tripping on the long skirt. "Let's go, Blue Blossom," he said.

14 "YOU GOTTA GET over Free Island idea, Java Jack," Bunga whispered as we went up the stairs. I had to go slow so my high heels wouldn't fall off. There was no point in trying to tell Bunga again that I didn't believe in Free Island politics. Bunga's whisper was something between a crash and a roar. "You gotta see what Fligh *is.* *True* Fligh."

Bunga opened the last door in the dark hallway upstairs. Behind the door was a maroon curtain made out of upholstery velvet. It smelled foul. Bunga pulled the curtain back.

I had to wait until my eyes adjusted to the darkness. There was one oil lamp with a green globe in the middle of a big round table. Shadowy shapes of men were hunched around it.

"True to form," said Fligh's smooth voice, "the Bugis comes late and brings a woman with him. Throw her out, Bunga."

Borneo Bill and Sulawesi Sue appeared, armed as usual. Bunga didn't budge. "Gentlemen, this my cousin, Blue Blossom," Bunga boomed out. "She speakee no English, only Chinee and Buginee. She stay, Bunga stay —she go, Bunga go. Flowers stick together."

Bunga's mocking pidgin imitation sharpened the tension in the dark room. One of the shadows at the table leaned toward another shadow, the one I guessed was Fligh, and whispered. Fligh sighed. Then his smooth hand snaked into the puddle of light around the lamp and

withdrew, leaving in the lamplight five enormous jewels
—red, white, green, blue, yellow.

I felt Bunga strain forward when the jewels appeared.
His eyes were staring. There was sweat on his forehead.

Fligh leaned forward into the lamplight. He was bare-
chested, and covered with scary tattooing.

"The girl can sit with Sulawesi Sue," Fligh ordered.
"Over there."

Sulawesi Sue grabbed me and shoved me back onto a
bench against the wall. She poked her pistol into my ribs.
I was sweating a lot. What if she tried to speak Chinese
to me?

Bunga had moved toward the table. He hadn't taken
his eyes off the jewels. The other men grouped around
the table had been drawn forward into the light too. It
was as if the gems had some fierce magnetic power. Now
I could see everybody clearly. One of the guys was
brown and fat. He had stars and braid and medals all over
his wet khaki uniform. He was wearing dark glasses.

The guy next to him was cleaning his ear with an
incredibly long fingernail. He was dressed in a plain
white shirt. His face was sallow and shiny with sweat.

"Nice to meet you, Bunga," the fat military guy said.
He extended his hand across the table toward Bunga.
"I've been trying to catch you for eight years. I just
missed you in Tolitoli last month, eh?"

Bunga started to inflate like a balloon. Thick cords of
muscle appeared in his neck, which was turning dark red.

"You Fligh punk, you," he said through his teeth,
"you say you need Bunga to pull big job—but you trick

me. Well, now you die."

I didn't know how Bunga intended to do it, but from the way he spoke, I was sure that in another minute everybody in the room, not just Fligh, was going to be dead. He half turned and gestured to me to get out. I rose and felt Sulawesi Sue's gun in my ribs.

"General Mambo is *with* us, not against us," Fligh intoned.

"General Pig Mambo killed too many good pirates," Bunga said as he strode to the curtain. On the way he grabbed my wrist, flipped me away from Sulawesi Sue, and slapped the gun out of her hand. It took less than a second.

"Listen to Pig Mambo for one minute," the guy in the white shirt rasped.

"One minute," Bunga said. "Then *everybody* die."

The general was all flustered. He kept dabbing his face with a white handkerchief. "The governments are closing the straits, Bugis. They've set up the pirate patrol. Ten ships already—ten more this year—all gunboats. They're all out to get you."

"Big deal," Bunga said.

"Yes!" the general shouted. "They have two destroyers, radar, money for bribes, an airplane—and all to get you!"

"So?"

"So," Fligh broke in, "General Mambo, Mr. Tsang, and I offer you the following. First, a share in the magnificent treasure of Maggasang—"

"Proof," Bunga said.

"In a moment," Fligh continued. "First, a share in the treasure. Next, free seas from Manila to Kalimantan for now, Irian and Java in five years' time."

"Fligh, I know you crazy," Bunga said, "so Bunga is not surprised to hear any of this. You got more to say, or ready to die now?"

"In return," Fligh went on, "you, Bunga, and your fleet will invade Timor—just to decoy the pirate patrol until we've finished mopping up in Maggasang."

"You talk like movie, crazy Fligh," Bunga said. "Five stones on that table—where the rest?"

"Strange you should ask," Fligh said. He snapped his fingers. Borneo Bill's behind moved into the room. He was walking backward, dragging a limp body. It turned out to be a thin old man. As Borneo Bill made his backward entrance, Tolitoli Tim quickly tied Fligh to his chair and smeared some makeup on his face. It was quick work —maybe thirty seconds—and Fligh suddenly looked as though he'd been given a terrible beating, with bruises and blood and everything. He looked as though he was going to die any moment.

The old guy they'd dragged in didn't look much better. The second he saw Fligh he started screaming, "Amin! Amin! Amin, my son!"

Fligh was—or the old fellow thought he was—his son! This was hard to believe. I'd never thought of Fligh as someone who had a father. He didn't seem like the sort of person who'd ever been born. Hatched, maybe.

The old man moaned and wailed and turned and twisted in his captor's grasp. They wouldn't let him get too close to Fligh, who just sat there looking beaten up. "Amin! Amin! You are alive!" the old guy cried. Tears were streaming down his cheeks. Tears were rolling out of Fligh's eyes too—probably something Tolitoli Tim had squirted into them.

Sulawesi Sue and Tolitoli Tim held Fligh at knife- and gun-point. Tolitoli Tim kept drawing the knife blade across Fligh's throat. This upset the old guy no end. "I will tell you! I will tell you!" he wailed. "Only spare my son!"

Tsang stood up and pointed his long nails at the old man. "Then tell."

The old man began to babble, sometimes incoherently, but clearly enough that I could get most of his tale. It had been a number of years back, he'd forgotten just how long, when he'd been called upon by the Sultan of Maggasang to accompany him and some other men on a secret journey. The sultan had blindfolded the men and made them travel for days and days, on foot, by ship, maybe even by plane—the old man's telling was confused—and then the blindfolds came off. There were five old men, one representing each of the major religious communities of Maggasang: Old Ishak, the Muslim haji; Budhi, the Buddhist teacher; Father Teorema, the Jesuit; Old Satirappa, the Balinese Hindu seer; and this guy, Old Gon, the *dukun*—the Dyak witch doctor.

The sultan made the old men swear never to tell what they were going to witness. They swore according to their faiths. Then the sultan blindfolded them again and led them someplace dark and cold. When they were allowed to see again, they found that they were standing in a cavern filled with precious stones—rubies, diamonds, emeralds, sapphires, topazes—and gold, lots of gold. Each of the old men was asked to perform prayers according to his religion, and then each was allowed to take five stones away with him.

Now, except for Old Gon and Budhi, all the men were dead. Nobody knew where Budhi was. Gon had hidden his jewels, but Amin—Fligh—had found them, and had stolen them when he ran away from home.

"There! There you see the stones!" the old man cried. "Now spare my son Amin!"

Fligh couldn't hide a look of fierce satisfaction—a sort of thrill passed over his face. "Take him away," he said, and, standing, he wiped the makeup from his smooth face. His tattoo rippled as he moved his muscles.

The old man gasped, "Amin!"

Fligh turned around. The tattoo on his back was just as ghastly. A black and green python with red eyes and a forked tongue wound its way along Fligh's arm and formed a big coil in the middle of his chest. A red and black dragonfly with green eyes spread its wings across Fligh's shoulders and onto his arms, while its narrow body ran down his spine and met the snake's tail, which was wrapped around his narrow waist.

Borneo Bill dragged the old man off. He was obviously dead before he reached the maroon curtain. Fligh had frightened his own father to death—although the beating the old man had had must have helped. However, he had convinced everybody there, including Blue

Blossom, of the existence of a great treasure somewhere.

Was it the treasure of the Invisible Hunter, the giant guardian? I wondered. Was it really on Maggasang, or was it on Equator? Fligh was not likely to tell everything he knew, even to his partners in crime.

"Where is this treasure?" Bunga asked.

"I do not know," Fligh replied, "but I *think* I know. It will take me a month or two to find out for sure. In the meantime, we will keep things going as usual. The F.I.M. raids will continue, just to keep people a little nervous, pirate forays will keep people distracted, and Tong smuggling will keep people worried about foreign powers. . . ."

"And when Fligh has found out for certain where the treasure is kept, he will let us know—won't you, Fligh?" Mambo said.

Fligh nodded. Tsang continued, "Then you Bugis will make phony attacks on Timor to decoy the pirate patrol, and we will close in on Maggasang."

"So treasure is here? On Maggasang?" Bunga asked.

"I think so—but it will be hard to get at," Fligh said.

I was getting pretty excited by this point. I was pretty sure that Fligh didn't know about Equator—that it was some big secret. He was getting Maggasang mixed up with Equator, where the treasure really was. The legend Munah told me said so. All these crafty crooked guys, killers and pirates, and I knew the secret—I had the piece of the puzzle they were missing. What was more, if I could get to Equator and find my mother and father, I just might find the treasure, not to mention pick up some of those jewels.

I had to talk to Bunga about this. I knew he didn't like Fligh—to put it mildly. I could imagine the laugh he was going to get out of it all. I wanted to get him out of there and talk it over with him. I tried my Chinese-girl voice: *"Shei-shei."*

Everybody in the room stared at me.

Bunga went white as a sheet. "Yah," he stammered, "yah, yah, Blue Blossom. I think Blue Blossom got sick stomach—gotta go."

Fligh's thin hand shot out and grabbed Bunga's arm. "Not so fast, Bugis."

Bunga's eyebrows beetled. He glared at Fligh.

Fligh peered at me. "The girl stays," he said. "A sign of your good faith."

"You want Bunga make phony invasion on Timor, you keep hands off Blue Blossom!"

"Tell me, Tuan Batik Pirate," Fligh sneered, "what is so precious about Miss Blue Blossom? My curiosity is aroused by her flawless Cantonese accent!"

I had done it. Bunga had almost pulled it off, and I'd gone and ruined it with my big mouth. I wouldn't have blamed Bunga if he'd left me there as a sign of good faith to Fligh. I didn't know then how deep a Bugis' loyalty goes once he's declared his friendship.

"You touch Blue Blossom and you die," Bunga boomed. "Blue Blossom Bugis woman, even if she talk Chinese—and Bunga's cousin beside. But I tell you what —you want proof, Bunga kill Blue Blossom himself, how about that?"

"That suits me," General Mambo said. "Let's see you do it."

"Ah, Bugis, my dear old boogeyman," said Fligh, "I take it, then, that your answer to the entire plan is yes?"

"Bunga gonna kill his cousin—make whole family mad—that good enough for you, Fligh?" Then he burst out laughing. He sauntered up to me and slapped my behind. "Batik Pirate say yes—say better kill what's yours with own hands."

Bunga shoved me through the maroon curtain and booted me out the door.

15   I LANDED IN a heap at the head of the stairs. My butt really hurt from Bunga's kick. He glowered at me, and then smiled his uneven white-toothed smile. Behind him, Borneo Bill and Sulawesi Sue poked their porky faces from behind the upholstery curtain.

"Fligh says move it, boogeyman," Borneo Bill said. "We'll watch you do the lady in—with your own hands."

Bunga wasn't paying any attention to Borneo Bill. He swayed on his flat feet. His hips and neck began to dance, and he did a kind of shuffle step back and forth. Borneo Bill and Sulawesi Sue tittered.

"Move it, boogeyman!"

Bunga swiveled and swayed. He began to sing in a big bass voice:

"Yawl kin keep yoh Muhammad Ali,
Yawl kin keep yoh Cassius Clay!
Yawl kin keep yoh ol' Joe Louis,
Yawl kin keep yoh Sugar Ray!
Cuz Ah'm da Batik Pirate,
An' honey, Ah knows da way,
T' dance da boogie-woogie
Da original boogeyman way!"

Bunga fixed me with crazy bugging eyes and shuffled toward me singing, "Do da boogie-woogie, boy, da original boogeyman way!" He sang that while he picked me up by the scruff of the neck and swung me under his arm. Upside down bobbed the faces of the F.I.M. kids, of Fligh, of Mambo and Tsang. I hoped my wig would stay put with all of Bunga's carrying on. I also hoped he wasn't going to kill me just to make his act *really* convincing.

"Bunga, you *are* mad," said Fligh in a condescending tone. "It's no wonder the English call you Bugis the boogeymen."

"Da boogeyman will get you if you don't watch out," Bunga sang as he danced down the stairs, carrying me. Between choruses, he muttered to me, "Just shut up and pretend you are Blue Blossom and not Java Jack, you hear? No more funny business!"

He crushed me in a big bear hug. I couldn't have said anything if I had wanted to. I was having a lot of trouble breathing.

Bunga crossed the floor of the Rumah Agung saloon,

singing while I turned blue in the face and kicked and struggled. Everybody laughed and hollered, "So long, Blue Blossom!"

"So long for good," snarled Borneo Bill.

We got out onto the sidewalk, with Bunga roaring, and me suffocating, and Borneo Bill and Sulawesi Sue following. I was fighting like mad to get a breath as we made our way to the waterfront. At one point I managed to get an eye free of Bunga's bulk and saw that we were surrounded by a lot of other boogeymen, probably Bunga's crew and men from other Bugis prahus.

I kept trying to tell Bunga to loosen up and let me breathe. His hand was tight across my mouth, on purpose. Bunga's smell and muscles and singing got worse. I couldn't stand it. It was like muddy water drowning me. I gathered all my strength to push myself away from the pirate and gulp air. I managed to do it.

I glimpsed the needle. It had fallen out the top of my dress. It had grown! It was the size of a lead pencil, the regulation type you get in school. In the second that I was writhing around before Bunga crushed me back to his chest, the needle got into a position between us. The point was pressed against Bunga's chest, and the eye end was lodged in the middle of an "A" in my Java Jack brass medallion.

As Bunga pressed me to his body, the point of the needle penetrated his purple batik shirt and disappeared into the flesh over his heart.

My wail was muffled in his armpit.

To my horror and relief, he kept right on striding and

singing down to the docks, as if nothing had happened. I thought maybe I had imagined that the needle had grown. Maybe the wound was no more than a pinprick to this tough pirate. Or maybe it had grown and shrunk again. At any rate, Bunga seemed to be all right.

But then I felt a faint slackening in Bunga's muscles. I pushed myself away from him and the needle slid out, covered with blood.

Bunga saw the needle. Borneo Bill and Sulawesi Sue saw the needle. The Bugis pirates around us saw the needle.

Bunga's eyes got bigger and bigger until they looked like saucers.

His words slowed down—he sounded like an old windup Victrola when the clockwork runs down. "Daaah . . . booo . . . gey . . . maaan'll get . . . you . . . ifff . . ."

Bunga's arms fell. I crashed to the dock.

Bunga pitched over the edge of the dock and thudded down to the deck of his prahu like a stone.

16 "BUNGAAAAA!" I CRIED.
My voice cracked. I flung myself from the wharf down onto the deck beside Bunga's lifeless body.

"Bunga!" the pirates cried in a chorus.

Through my tears I saw a solid circle of Bugis sailors closing in on me.

Borneo Bill and Sulawesi Sue stood on the dock.

"Well, well!" Borneo Bill smirked down at me. "Looks like Bunga's boys will do his work for him. Come on, Sulawesi Sue, let the Bugis do the dirty work. I want a beer." And they left.

"Maybe he's not dead," I said to the Bugis. "Let's get a doctor."

Nobody listened to me. They just kept coming closer, angry, ugly, brandishing krises, knives, and clubs. Somebody had gotten behind me and made to slash my throat. He grabbed my long black hair, intending to pull my head back so he could make his cut. The wig came off.

The Bugis howled. They all jumped back. It must have surprised them to see my yellow hair in the moonlight. I tore off the Chinese dress. Underneath I was wearing blue jeans cut off at the knees. I wiped the sweat off my face with the dress, and a lot of my Blue Blossom makeup came off.

The Bugis gasped again when they saw my black face. Then they started laughing. My being a kid didn't seem to matter to them. They settled right down to the business of getting even with me for murdering Bunga.

They approached, holding the krises and sticks out in front of them. They didn't make a sound. Something told me that there was no point in my making a noise either. I hadn't seen any evidence of police in Maggasang. Screaming would probably just bring more pirates. They were going to make short work of me, and my choice was to just take it or fight.

I decided to fight. I got strangely calm. I figured that as long as I was going to join Bunga, I might as well do it in style.

So I laughed. I tried to laugh the sort of laugh that Errol Flynn made in the movies—sort of devil-may-care. But it didn't come out sounding like Errol Flynn's laugh. It sounded hysterical and loony. It stopped the Bugis in their tracks. They looked at me and at each other. Then I stuck out my left hand like a traffic cop. Stop. They stopped. While I held them at bay with my outstretched palm, I fumbled for my needle and slipped the chain over my head.

The needle was still as long as a pencil and covered with Bunga's blood. I wiped the blood off on my jeans and held it up in the moonlight. It gleamed gold.

The Bugis murmured.

I whipped the needle around like a sword. I jumped in the air, spread my legs and came down straddling Bunga's body.

Some Bugis lunged at me with their curving krises. My arm went into fast action, warding off the stabbing they tried to do.

I was lucky. The needle had incredible strength for something so skinny. It didn't slip around in my hand, either. One of the Bugis krises snapped when it hit the needle. Another one plunked out of the owner's hand and landed on the deck.

All I knew about this kind of fighting was what I had seen on the late movies—*The Count of Monte Cristo* and *The Crimson Pirate,* things like that. I'd never dreamed it would be so easy to hold off a flock of pirates, let alone with a needle six inches long.

The Bugis got more enthusiastic. The needle was whacking away like a broadsword. It was a beautiful slasher. Somehow, I could never get it to cut anybody. I got cut and scratched a dozen times, but I couldn't seem to score a hit on even one of the boogeymen. Once I had a perfect chance to stick somebody in the stomach, but as I thrust the needle forward, I felt it veer to the left at the last moment. As a result of that mishap I got cut across the right shoulder. I was getting the distinct feeling that it wasn't me at all doing the fighting. It was the needle. It was weird. The needle seemed to have the knack of getting me and my arm into the right position at the exact moment to knock somebody's kris out of order, but it wouldn't hurt anybody. Notwithstanding, it had killed my friend Bunga.

Generally speaking, I am not very interested in magic. Aunt Amy raised me to be very suspicious of things like that. And ray guns and whatnot leave me cold. Still, there was no doubt that there was something distinctly magical about this needle.

My arm was beginning to tire. I switched hands, even though I'm all thumbs as a lefty. My awkwardness didn't have any effect on the needle's performance. Maybe thirteen or fourteen Bugis had tried their hands and retreated, mostly without weapons. At first the men grumbled and cursed, but then somebody broke out laughing. That was when the needle knocked the double krises out of the hands of one pockmarked fellow with crossed eyes. It must have looked funny.

More Bugis started chuckling. Then my big break

came. They started betting. That meant that only one pirate at a time would fight me and the needle. That made it easier for me—but at the same time, all the Bugis not fighting could rest. I suppose they were all getting tired, but they couldn't have been as tired as I was.

My arms were feeling numb, like they'd already dropped off, but the needle was feeling fine, and it dragged me along after it.

It beat a tall, scar-faced monster with a black bandana on.

It spun a fancy-prancing young Bugis with a bowie knife right off the deck and into the bay.

It disarmed the fleet's number-one kris man.

By that time, the boogeymen were cheering and whistling and slapping one another's backs. I was out of breath, panting, wiping the sweat off my face and chest. I staggered this way and that, and the Bugis seemed to go crazy. They stood up and roared.

Then all at once they went silent. All I could hear was my own breathing and heartbeat.

I looked at the deck and saw a huge shadow come up behind me. Another attacker. I flexed my arm, but the needle hung like a dead weight in my hand. It wouldn't move. I looked at it.

It weighed a ton. I could hardly hold on to it.

And it had shrunk back to its original size—it was hardly two inches long!

The shadow had its hands on my shoulders. The shadow was talking. It had a big bass voice that wobbled at first and then got stronger until it boomed out over the bay. It was talking in Buginese.

"Men of Manado! Men of Tolitoli! Men of Longalla! Men of Tomini! Men of Tinombo! Men of Butung and Banda! Listen! Listen, for I am Bunga the Bugis, the Batik Pirate! Let every man know that this one with the yellow hair and black face is forever under my protection. Whoever, from this moment, harms this one, or offers to harm him—that man shall know the anger of Bunga. Let everyone know that this is my little brother —and his name is Java Jack!"

The Bugis cheered.

Bunga was towering behind me silhouetted by the squashed yellow moon, his purple silk shirt drenched in blood from the needle wound. He was smiling his crooked white-toothed smile and holding on to my shoulders for dear life so he wouldn't fall over again. He said in English, "Dah needleman will get you if you don't watch out!"

The Bugis cheered again.

"But it takes more than a needle to get the boogeyman!"

"Bunga!" I whooped. "You're alive!"

The pirates were going crazy.

Then Bunga held up his hand for silence. "Now we sail," he said softly, speaking in Buginese, "each to his own wind, each to his own fate's keeping. But beware!" Bunga's voice dropped to a whisper. "Beware of the pirate patrol—gunboats all—and chart your courses carefully. Let us meet again two months from now in the Bay of Babar on the Night of the Crumbling Moon!" Bunga sounded funny when he talked in English, but in Buginese, he sounded just like a movie. "And may Allah and the blessings of the Prophet, Peace be upon Him, be with you in all your journeyings!"

One final cheer rose from the throats of the assembled Bugis, and then, with one accord, they began hoisting sails—enormous purple, brown, and black Bugis sails.

 **17** THE CREW OF Bunga's prahu, to my surprise, consisted of only three men. There was Bim, the scar-faced monster I'd fought, who was even bigger and broader than Bunga; Junah, the fancy-footwork guy with the bowie knife; and the number-one kris man, whose name was Yudis.

They scrambled into the rigging, Junah and Yudis, and unfurled the sails of Bunga's boat. The heavy blue canvas of the first sail fell open. It was batiked with a zillion colored flowers. The big center sail was purple. An enormous red and yellow flower, a kind of crazy rose, was batiked like a sun in the middle of the sail. The third sail was black and batiked in rainbow designs over a flower-covered mountain. The last sail was brown, just plain brown—unless you looked up close and saw that it was made up of hundreds of dark brown wedding batiks stolen from islands all over the archipelago.

The moon set. The dawn made the horizon blue, then green, then red. In the first light I could see that Bunga's prahu not only had ornate sails—it was decorated all over. The whole surface of the ship was carved and painted. Every corner, every plank, every nook and cranny was carved up with crazy curlicue and batik designs, and every kind of flower you can think of.

The island of Maggasang had vanished behind us. I hung over the bow, under the sail, looking to see if there was a nameplate. Sure enough, carved in red letters on a gold background was *The Boogeyman.*

Bunga was standing back on the high poop. He had his arms crossed over the big batik bandages Yudis had made for him.

"Bunga, where are we going?" I called to him.

"Where we go? Where you think?" he replied. "Show Bunga map."

I pulled Munah's crumpled batik map out of the back pocket of my jeans. I ran back, up to the poop deck, and gave it to Bunga. He smoothed it out and peered at it.

"Yah," he said, "we go to island of E-qua-tor!"

It was the end of the dry season. Typhoons were coming up soon. The winds were picking up, the waves were rising, and the sky was clear. It was great sailing weather.

For one week we sailed around in a circle north of Tolitoli, trying to figure out which of the ten-thousand-odd islands nearby was the one Munah had shown on the map as Equator.

We lay on our stomachs on the deck examining the huge fold-out navigator's chart Bunga had stolen a couple of years before from the Royal Brunei Navy Office.

It was a real official British map, with everything on it in every language. Every island had at least four names—the name the natives called it, the name the Dutch called it, the name the British called it, the name the Indonesians called it. Sometimes the official name was one of the four, but more often it wasn't. It drove me crazy.

In order to narrow the choices down to a thousand or so, I figured I'd better tell Bunga and the boogeymen everything I knew. I started with Neosho, and didn't leave anything out. They loved the story, and each of them would ask me to retell a favorite part of my adventure. There was plenty of time to talk. Life on a Bugis prahu going around in a circle isn't exactly busy. Everybody had jobs to do, of course, but most of them never got done. One of my jobs was bailing out water from the hold. Bugis boats are notorious leakers.

The main item of interest on board, however, was my needle.

"I wonder what the needle is made of that makes it act so strange," Yudis said. He spoke good English. He'd learned it in Kota Kinabalu from a retired English plantation owner.

"Maybe it's smelted from real meteor dust the way the ancient krises were, man," Junah said. He'd learned his English from the American hippies in Bali.

We all looked at the needle hanging innocently on the chain around my neck.

"Bunga think needle connected to Equator somehow," Bim said.

We kept on sifting through all the information we had

—about treasures, and my parents, and islands, and signs in the sky; about Fligh's father's story and the Invisible Hunter. We told and retold my story, and parts of the story that the boogeymen knew or had heard. In the end, everyone agreed with my original suspicion—that the treasure, the one Fligh was interested in, was on Equator, not on Maggasang.

Now that I think about it and know the Bugis a little better, it seems likely that we all reached that conclusion because that was the conclusion I wanted to reach. Bunga wanted to do what I wanted to do, so my conclusion was his conclusion. It's not logical, but the Bugis are like that.

We made a list of qualities the island we were looking for would have to have:

1. *A name that meant Equator, maybe in some ancient language.*

2. *Location on or near the equator.*

3. *Two prominent mountains in the middle, like the ones Munah had drawn on her map.*

4. *A round or roundish shape—again, as Munah had drawn.*

5. *A palace, preferably a water palace, whatever that was.*

6. *A legend of treasure—preferably jewels; gold okay; no sunken treasure admissible.*

7. *Not well known. (That was obvious, or we would have found it by now.)*

8.   *Somehow located so that the Sultan of Maggasang and
my parents could have gotten there—maybe meaning
that it wasn't too far away from Maggasang.*

Bunga, Bim, Junah, Yudis, and I took turns using the
Brunei Navy chart and making up lists of what each of
us thought were the ten most likely islands.

One island on everybody's list was called Chatulistiwa.
It was number six on my list and number one on Bunga's.
It was a little island seventy miles square. Its southern
edge was sitting smack-dab on the equator. It wasn't
Dutch, wasn't British, and hadn't yet become Indonesian. That suggested that maybe the Sultan of Maggasang
had contact with the Sultan of Chatulistiwa.

Bunga had met the Sultan of Chatulistiwa years ago at
a big banquet on Buru. His name was Kanabombom—
King Kanabombom.

The island's name, Chatulistiwa, was a word meaning
equator in ancient Arabic. Ancient Arabic took a lot of
words from Sanskrit, and Sanskrit was the basis of the
Maggasang language, so maybe that was the connection
with Munah's name for the island, Equator.

The British called the island Kanabombom, and the
Bugis called it the Island of the Weebos. Weebos are
related to the mouse deer, but they've got fat tails like
rabbits. The interesting thing about weebos is that they
collect shiny baubles and trinkets, as some birds do, to
decorate their nests. There was a legend of the Lost
Valley of the Weebos and the treasure of jewels and gold

the little animals had collected and brought there.

Another thing that attracted us to Chatulistiwa was a pair of fat mountains sitting on either side of a river.

The only bit of information that didn't fit came from Bunga. He said that the palace wasn't called the Water Palace, and that the island sometimes had water shortages.

But there was plenty of reason to suspect that Chatulistiwa might be the island of Equator, and we set our course for it.

We celebrated our decision by breaking out a bottle of Bugis wine. It was just a kind of fruit punch, but a bit sour. The Muslim Bugis aren't supposed to drink. Bunga went below and brought up his Bugis harp. Junah got out his guitar, and Yudis a Sundanese flute from Java. Bim beat a drum. They made beautiful Bugis music. They sang sad songs in Arabic, Malay, and Buginese. Then they began to thump out a familiar beat, and Bunga started in on "Original Boogeyman Boogie-Woogie." I joined in. We sang and hollered and danced and carried on until morning, while *The Boogeyman* sailed the Molucca Sea. At dawn the pirates washed their heads, noses, ears, mouths, legs, and arms, and did the Muslim morning prayers. Then we sat together while the sun came up, sipped coffee, and talked.

Bunga claimed that being stabbed by the needle had done him a world of good. He said it was like some sort of drastic acupuncture. He'd had heart pains before, but after he'd been stabbed by the needle, they'd stopped.

"Now I am health!" Bunga beamed.

"It's all true," Junah joined in. "Bunga was looking bad—his skin had lost its natural color. But after the needle got him, he got his color back!"

I had to take Junah's word for this, having only seen Bunga by lamplight and moonlight before he got needled.

"Bunga slow down too much," big Bim said slowly. He stood up and shadowboxed. "Now Bunga fast again!" Bim spun around and punched the air.

Bunga jumped up and took Bim on in a sparring match. They were both big Muhammad Ali fans. What Bim had been saying was that Bunga had started to get sluggish in their morning boxing sessions on deck.

Yudis confided next, "You know, Java Jack, I was really scared that Bunga would have a heart attack—that or a stroke—the way he'd rant and rave whenever he got mad. It's strange, isn't it? He's much quieter since the needle. . . ." Yudis pulled the needle out of my shirt. "I really wonder what this thing is made of. I hope we find your father. Maybe he'll know."

Bunga danced around us, imitating Ali. "Don't worry. We find Tuan Robinson! And then we find airplane, and Java Jack take Bunga flying!"

Bunga pranced off. Yudis smiled. "Bunga's had lots of chances to fly—but he never trusted pilots until you turned up."

"I no fly except Java Jack take me up!" Bunga panted. "Look!" He gestured around at the rushing blue-green waves. "In sea you can swim if prahu goes down—but sky?"

"You can jump out with a parachute, Bunga," I said.

"Yah, and if only one parachute in plane?" he teased, reminding me of Fligh's exit from the Cessna.

Absentmindedly, I reached over and picked up Bunga's harp. It was made of wood inlaid with silver stars and sunbursts, and it had twelve strings. Traces of paint remained on the bowlike, curved frame. There had once been bands of red, yellow, blue, green, purple. I remembered Munah's poem. I remembered it as a song, and tried to pick it out on the harp. My nails were short, not long and tough like Bunga's, and I couldn't get the thing to work. I slid the needle off the chain and used it as a pick, strumming with it.

The sound was fantastic. It sounded like ten harps and guitars rolled into one. Bunga stopped boxing and grinned. He watched my fingers and got a strange look on his face. The others were watching and staring too.

I looked at the needle. It had grown—was growing.

In a couple of minutes it was as long as an arrow. It even looked like an arrow. The eye end had a notch like an arrow's.

I tried it out—the notch against a harp string. It fit perfectly. I raised the harp and stretched the needle-arrow across it. It was crazy, what I was going to do. We were out in the middle of the Molucca Sea, and if I missed my target, the precious thing would be gone for good.

But I really couldn't help it. It was as though the needle insisted on getting shot out of that bow-shaped harp.

So I held my breath, and Bunga held his breath, and
the rest of the boogeymen held their breath, and I drew
the harp string taut.

I let the needle fly. It zinged across the twelve strings
and left a music in the air like nothing any of us had ever
heard. It sounded like an organ—an organ so high-
pitched that only dogs and spirits could hear most of it.
It was probably a good thing we couldn't hear more of
the strange music—it would have driven us all crazy, like
the sirens' song. The strings went on ringing for maybe
a minute, maybe ten minutes. We were all frozen.

Meanwhile, the needle had sunk, dead center, into the
mainmast, where I'd aimed it. By the time the ringing
came to an end and we all had shaken ourselves out of
our shock, the needle had shrunk again. It was hard to
find and dig out, the mast being covered as it was with
all that fancy, colored carving.

18 IT WAS NO wonder that old Ibu told me
some guys would kill to get ahold of that
needle she'd made. I'd bet that if it
hadn't been for Bunga, there would
have been some fighting right on board
The Boogeyman over who was going to keep that hunk of
magic metal.

You could see Bim's big black eyes glowing when he

held the needle in his hands. He tried to hide what he was feeling by lowering his thick black bandana down over his forehead, but it was obvious.

Junah was different. He tried to get the needle to do things, as if it were a puppy to teach tricks to. The needle didn't do anything but lie in front of Junah, no matter what he said or how he concentrated his willpower on it.

"I don't think it works like magic," I said to Junah.

"Then how does it work, smart guy?" he fumed.

"I don't know, Junah, but I think it's *programmed* to do what it does—sort of like—well—certain kinds of cells are programmed to turn into certain kinds of plants. The DNA molecules. It's all genetics—you know what I mean?"

"Magic," murmured Bim.

Yudis had the most success with the needle. He just picked it up and started to write with it on a piece of paper as if it were a ball-point pen. Yudis was no dummy. The letters he wrote on the paper appeared in green ink —a couple of minutes after he'd written them.

"It does invisible writing too!" I exclaimed. "How'd you know, Yudis?"

"I kept my eyes open, Java Jack. I saw traces of green on Bunga's wound, and later on the mast when we dug the needle out."

Bunga didn't want to handle the needle, or try to do tricks with it. "It belong to Sultan of Equator. Maybe that my friend, King Kanabombom. Up to when King Kanabombom get needle in his hand, better I don't touch. Better just Java Jack."

That ended our fooling with the needle. Bunga didn't have to give orders to his men, or even make suggestions. As soon as they knew how he felt about something, they acted as though they felt the same, whether they did or not.

Bunga spent a lot of time sitting on the deck and staring at nothing.

"What are you thinking about, Bunga?" I asked him a few hours after he'd spoken to the boogeymen and me about playing with the needle.

"Pirate," he said, "Bunga think about pirate. All pirate sailing sea everywhere." Bunga didn't say any more.

There was something on his mind, and it wasn't long before his loyal crewmen noticed it.

"Do you know what's the matter with Bunga, Java Jack?" Junah asked me the next day. "He *looks* okay, but I think his mind's beginning to wander."

"Sometime better mind wander, Junah!" Bunga boomed. He'd come up behind us without our hearing him and was standing behind us with the wind whipping his batik shirt. "One day more, and we see Chatulistiwa —Equator island. Made good time, real good."

My hair was curling down around my ears, and the sun had bleached it yellower than ever. My face must have been darker than ever too. Bunga gave me some of his old clothes, since my jeans wouldn't be enough when we got to Chatulistiwa.

"You gotta look nice to meet father and King Kanabombom," Bunga said. Together we cut down a pair of his green velvet pants, and I sewed them up with some yellow silk cord Bunga had taken from a Singhalese schooner in the Bay of Bengal. He gave me a couple of plain white Indian cotton shirts and a beautiful piece of brocade stitched in red, white, and blue. "America colors, you know?" Bunga said. "Make nice belt." There weren't any mirrors on board *The Boogeyman,* but I figured I looked okay from the way everybody clapped when I finally got everything sewn together and tried the outfit on. I'd used my needle for sewing, and it had worked fine. It didn't do any magic, just sewed—although I'd have traded the trick with the harp for anything that would have made my sewing job easier.

In fact, I got to be a pretty good sewer, and everybody brought me ripped and worn stuff to mend. So I sat at the base of the mainmast and set up a seagoing tailor shop. I wondered if these pirates were putting me on—after all, all the sewing I'd ever done was in making my cut-down boogeyman suit. Maybe they were just pretending to be impressed with my skill so someone would do their mending for them. For my part, I didn't care. I was really happy to do something for those guys.

"Hey! Sail to starboard!" Junah cried from the top of the mast. Yudis, Bim, and I stood up and craned our necks to see, but it was still a speck. Bunga didn't budge. He sat on the deck and stared in the opposite direction.

"Bunga! Bunga!" Bim and Junah shouted. "What do we do? She's a Canton junk—bet she's loaded."

Bunga blinked. He turned around and shaded his eyes. "Yah," he sighed. "Must be loaded."

He dragged himself to his feet and yawned. He

shrugged at me. "Gotta go to work, Java Jack. You go down. Better you not see."

I didn't want to go below. I wanted to help the rest of the pirates hold up the junk, and I told Bunga so.

"Java Jack! You don't do anything! You want to watch, okay—you sit still." Bunga had never hollered at me before. I didn't feel like giving him an argument. "And don't make with needle! Understand?" I understood.

Yudis turned us to windward and we bore down on the Chinese junk. She was a big one, and slow. I had always heard all this talk about how junks are the world's finest sailing ships. They aren't. They can't maneuver, they roll and pitch like bucking broncos, and they're easy to catch.

This junk sailed like a cow walking through a pasture. The sails were thick and orange and yellow. They were all flapping sideways so you couldn't see behind the junk. When we got within five hundred yards they hoisted a white flag—just like in the movies. Bunga, Bim, Junah, and Yudis got out their pistols, knives, and krises.

We pulled up alongside. The captain was bowing and talking pidgin Malay. *"Selamat datang, Tuan-tuan,"* he babbled, "welcome aboard, my lords!" I guessed he was used to being held up. The idea was to be very polite and give the pirates just enough of the cargo so they'd be satisfied and wouldn't go looking for the *really* valuable stuff. The crew of the junk all bowed along with the captain—there must have been thirty of them, all shapes and sizes, plus lots of kids and their mothers. I could see cooking pots and laundry hung out to dry. The junk was a floating apartment house.

"What cargo you carry?" Bunga asked.

"Poor cargo, very poor." The captain bowed and scraped. He snapped his fingers. "Ah-Fei, go fast bring the Tuan samples of our cargo." One of the sailors hurried behind the wall of sails.

Bunga and Bim were standing with the junk captain, while Junah and Yudis had clambered to either end of the junk and stood poised with krises in their teeth and pistols in their hands, watching everything that went on. Ah-Fei scurried out from a crack in the wall of sail. He was carrying bolts of colored silk and shiny round tins, and a bunch of little boxes. The crack between sails he came through flapped open a couple of times after him. I did a double take. There were lots of guys in khaki uniforms with machine guns lined up on the other side of the sails. The sun was coming from our side so you couldn't see their shadows. Bobbing on the far side of the junk was a gray mast—there was a military ship, a fast cutter, concealed behind the junk.

It was the pirate patrol! This was a trap! I had to do something to warn Bunga and the others—but I couldn't risk alarming anybody. I wanted to yell, but I was afraid the soldiers would start shooting.

I grabbed Bunga's harp, pulled out my needle, and began strumming madly and singing at the top of my lungs.

"Dah boogeyman'll get you if you don't watch out!" I sang. "Dah boogeyman'll get you if you don't watch out!"

I sang and stamped my foot, and sweated and prayed.

The Chinese junk folk were drawn toward the sound of the harp. They'd never heard anything like my needle harp-playing before—nobody had. The captain tried to shoo them back, but they all crowded to the rail and looked down at me playing and singing on the deck of the prahu.

Bunga's expression started out annoyed. He began to get angry, but then, when I didn't stop playing even after he'd given me an unmistakable signal, he stopped moving and sniffed the air. He looked like a bird dog on a point. He'd caught the gunboat smell on a change of wind.

"Here very nice silk, very nice spice, very nice gem. You like, Tuan?" The junk captain spread all the stuff the sailor had brought on the deck in front of Bunga.

In a booming loud voice that could be heard for miles, Bunga said, "Nah! We don't feel like buying any this stuff—thanks just the same, captain. And, captain! Everybody! Listen! Listen to big new rock 'n' roll star—Java Jack!"

By this time Bim, Junah, and Yudis had caught on. They casually hopped back onto the prahu and picked up their instruments. They started playing.

Bunga bellowed again, "Last week Java Jack big smash hit singer in Tolitoli. Next week big smash hit opening at Bugis Street Bandstand in Singapore. I am Bunga the Bugis, the Batik Pirate, you know?"

"Yes, yes, Tuan, we know," the captain babbled.

I saw a couple of the soldiers peeping around the edges of the sails.

"I am the Batik Pirate, and I tell you all, you people —you better come hear Java Jack and dah Boogeymen next time, you know?"

Just then the wind shifted and the sails of the junk whipped around. There was nobody minding them, the Chinese crew having come to the side to listen to the new rock group, the Boogeymen. There were about twenty-five guys with machine guns, all tapping their toes to "The Boogeyman Boogie-Woogie."

Bunga smiled his biggest smile. "Hey, pirate patrol guys! How you do? Big Pig Mambo send you? Yaah-hooo!" Bunga whooped, and he leaped to the deck of the prahu. "I tell you gun boys, you come hear us in Kota Kinabalu!"

Bunga pushed the prahu away from the side of the junk and joined me in singing while Junah, Yudis, and Bim got us under way. Bunga waved. The junk captain and the junk families waved back. The soldiers looked confused at first, as if they didn't know what to do, and then they waved too. "See you all in Kota Kinabalu!"

"That was beautiful!" I cried to Bunga.

"You do fast thinking too!" Bunga laughed.

Junah wiped his forehead. "I'm glad that's over with!"

"Bunga touch one finger on junk cargo, and machine guns blow us all up," said Bim.

"Either that or jail in Manila until we rot," said Yudis.

"Oh, Bunga, I have to hand it to you—what a sense of

humor! Imagine us, a bunch of pirates, playing rock 'n' roll in Kota Kinabalu!"

"Maybe," Bunga said, "and maybe we play—Bunga has to think, but Bunga thinks maybe he gave his word."

 19 CHATULISTIWA WAS A bust. King Kanabombom was up-country. Nobody had ever heard of my folks. Nobody had ever heard of Maggasang. There wasn't any such thing as a Water Palace. There *was* a water shortage. And Chatulistiwa wasn't round.

"British map made fifty years ago," the Chatulistiwa librarian told me, "before big earthquake. Half island sink. Poof. Lotta peoples say Lost Valley and weebo treasure go with it."

Chatulistiwa was definitely *not* the island of Equator. And we were broke.

Bunga toyed with the idea of going into the weebo smuggling business, but he was really too kindhearted to massacre thousands of defenseless animals just to send their tails to South America to be made into sofa cushions. In fact, none of the usual forms of crime appealed to Bunga. He moped around the cheap hotel and waited for Bim, Junah, and Yudis to bring him some scheme that sounded appealing. All Bunga would have had to do was say the word, and bags full of money or whatever he wanted would have been brought to him at once by some

Chinese trader or would-be smuggler anxious to gain some advantage in the cutthroat business of sailing the seas.

A couple of times exactly that happened, and Bunga kicked the guys out into the street—really, not a figure of speech.

After three days, Bunga decided he was hungry. He had given up eating when our hopes of Chatulistiwa being Equator gave out—all he had done was drink cup after cup of jasmine tea.

So Bunga took us all down to the big sailor hangout for a meal. There was a dinky bar, and lots of beat-up metal tables and folding chairs under a tent roof. There was a microphone for making announcements. This restaurant catered to spur-of-the-moment sailor weddings. It seemed Chatulistiwa girls wouldn't even go out on a date with a guy unless he married them first—that's what Junah told me. Anyway, Bunga spotted that microphone. Nothing would do but that I sing so Bunga could hear how it sounded with a real microphone.

It sounded good. The Chatulistiwa crowd went crazy. We did about ten encores of "The Original Boogeyman Boogie-Woogie."

One thing led to another, and Bunga had booked us into a saloon in Manado.

En route we stopped off at five islands that might possibly be Equator. On one of them there weren't even any people—just some enormous lizards the size of rhinos. Some people call them Komodo dragons, but Bunga insisted they were runaways from Chatulistiwa and were

properly called Kanabombom dragons after the king
who'd first found them. We gave them a concert while
they sunned themselves and stared at us with lidless eyes.
After that performance, we were ready for any kind of
audience. Bunga said, "Now ready for Kota Kinabalu."

Two weeks later, our act opened at the Kota Kinabalu
Roxy. We were billed as "Java Jack and the Batik Pirate
with the Boogeyman Band." We were sold out in advance. The Roxy was a movie house, and before our
performance they screened *Captain Blood*—a scratchy old
print with three rows of subtitles.

Yudis and Junah were of the opinion that the crowd
had showed up because the Batik Pirate had ordered
them to. Bim thought they were probably curious. I
agreed with both opinions, but Bunga was sure: "They
come because we great rock band, you know?"

Even after our triumphs in Chatulistiwa and Manado,
I wasn't in the least convinced that we were great. Here
in the big city they'd laugh in our faces.

Well, the Kota Kinabalu crowd went wild. We
couldn't go out in the street without being mobbed by
kids. We were held over for four days, and could have
stayed longer, but Bunga met some kind of a theatrical
agent who offered us a ten-week contract in Hong Kong
at the disco in the Mandarin Hotel.

"Too far north," Bunga said, and tore up the contract.
"How about Balikpapan?"

"Mister Bunga, sir," the agent said, "they don't have
a night club in Balikpapan, much less a disco!"

"Better make one," Bunga said, and he shut the guy out of the room.

 **20** THIRTY-SEVEN ISLANDS, six major cities, fifty-three concerts, and seven records later—also one hundred thousand T-shirts, half a million posters, twelve-thousand-odd autographs, and sixty thousand fan letters later—and fifty-nine days after leaving Maggasang Bay, we were heading from Jakarta to Babar. Babar is the biggest island between Timor and Tanimbar, and we were heading there for our rendezvous with the Bugis fleet on the Night of the Crumbling Moon.

We were flying.

We'd left *The Boogeyman* in dry dock for refitting in Singapore. It was being wired for sound and light. During our performance in Balikpapan we had used the boat as a stage. We had done a half-baked job of converting *The Boogeyman* to a sort of showboat, but the audiences had loved it. Now we were letting the professionals do the job right.

They were also rigging a new mainsail for us. Instead of a rose, it was going to have a copy of Munah's batik —not the map part, just the drawing of the rainbow, the mountains, the stars, and the comet. That was to be identified with one of our hit songs, "Rainbow." I had lifted

the words from Munah's poem about the Invisible
Hunter.

> *"His bow is the bow of the rainy day,*
> *His strap is the moon growing old.*
> *His bow is strung with the Milky Way,*
> *His arrow a comet of gold."*

Our greatest hit, of course, was "The Original
Boogeyman Boogie-Woogie."

Bunga had bought the plane without telling anybody.
We always left the money stuff to Bunga. He made the
deals as he'd always done. All we had to do was turn up
onstage to play and sing.

Bunga spent the advance money from a record album
deal he'd made to buy the plane. It was an old DC-3 that
had been totally restored and fitted out with pontoons as
well as wheels, so it could land on water. It was better
than new, and shiny bright. The outside had a nifty blue
and white paint job—official airline style—with a band of
batik figures around the middle. The inside was super-
deluxe. It was really a neat airplane. With the plane,
Bunga hired a professional pilot. This was just for show
—it was going to be my job to fly the DC-3, but we
needed someone with a license, now that we were making officially reported flights, and it's always a good idea
to have a copilot along. The pilot's name was Benjie. He
was a nice guy, but he didn't really want to fit in. It was
just a job to him. So we mostly ignored him, and he
mostly ignored us.

The boogeymen were enjoying our stunning success as entertainers. That is, Bim, Junah, and Yudis were having a good time. About Bunga it was hard to tell. He had gotten awfully dignified—for him—since he'd become an impresario. As for me, I was sad. In fact, I was about ready to chuck the whole business and go back to Neosho.

What depressed me was this. Here we were, famous all over Southeast Asia. We were on the radio hundreds of times a day. Our concerts were sold out. Everybody in this part of the world knew who we were. So where were my parents? My only hope was that my mother and father might be someplace where there wasn't a TV or a radio, or a kid who liked music—if such a place still existed.

Bunga knew I was feeling miserable. That was the main reason he'd bought the airplane—to cheer me up. It did, too, a little.

With the airplane we could step up our island search. This was good, because, so far, we'd found nothing. Still, there were thousands and thousands of islands left.

My worst day as a rock 'n' roll star was our farewell parade down Thamrin Boulevard in Jakarta, from the Senayan Stadium. Fifty thousand screaming kids—it all seemed meaningless. We were riding on a papier mache replica of *The Boogeyman.* There were fifty-foot posters of us lining the road. There were Java Jack and Batik Pirate shirts. And everybody was doing the original boogeyman boogie-woogie. It was all so stupid, without finding my parents.

I cheered up a bit on board the plane, which had been named, of course, *The Flying Boogeyman.*

Bunga came on board late, with two passengers. One was an old guy with a batik turban and a scraggly white beard. The other guy was his servant.

"Old Bapak Joya ask if we take him to Babar too," Bunga said. "He cousin to headman there. Bunga say, sure! Come!"

"Fine, Bunga," I answered. "Just be sure to show Bapak Joya the seat belt and the life jacket procedures, okay?"

We had thirty-five parachutes on board, and Bunga had personally inspected every one.

I pulled out the chart of the region we were flying over and circled all the likely islands—ones that might be Equator. There were nearly thirty of them between Bali and the Banda Sea.

Benjie, the hired pilot, grumbled from the back of the cabin, "More island-hopping? You guys are crazy. You'll never find that imaginary island. Even if it existed, it would be a needle in a haystack."

Benjie went off to sleep in the passenger section. He was right, or course. It was hopeless. But what else could I do? I turned over the engines. Bunga came in and belted himself into the copilot's seat. Clearance came through. We took off.

"Java Jack," Bunga whispered after the takeoff lights had gone out. I looked over at him. He was looking bad all of a sudden. His face was hanging and his eyes were bloodshot.

"Bunga! What's wrong with you?" I asked.

"Bunga needs to ask Java Jack's advice."

"*My* advice?"

Bunga rubbed his eyes with his big brown hands. "Bunga don't know what to do," he said. He held out a yellow paper he'd been folding and refolding all day. I knew what it was—an interisland telegram. We'd gotten lots of them since becoming stars. I took the paper and read:

BUNGA BATIK PIRATE
BOROBUDUR HOTEL JAKARTA

CONGRATULATIONS NEW CAREER. HOPE
DOES NOT INTERFERE TIMOR TRAVEL PLANS
ON 18TH.
> TANGO

"Tango?" I asked. Before Bunga answered I knew who Tango was—Tsang and Mambo, Fligh's partners in crime. Tango.

"Fligh ready for invasion on Maggasang. Cable come alla time." Bunga pulled a wad of similar telegrams from Tango out of his pocket. I looked at my watch calendar. It was already the sixteenth.

"So?" I said. "Who cares what those guys want?"

"Bunga cares. Bunga made promise, Java Jack. Say yes to Fligh. Big mistake. Bugis never break word—better break neck."

"But, Bunga," I said.

"Yah, Bunga know what Java Jack gonna say—Bunga no more pirate. Bunga the big pirate dead—killed!" He looked at the needle hanging around my neck. "Needle kill Bunga the pirate. Ever since that time, make me sick, killing, robbing, bad stuff. But what Bunga do now? What Bunga the Bugis gonna do—run away?"

"Look, Bunga," I said, "I don't think anybody has to keep a promise to a guy like Fligh and those other rats."

"Yah, and then Bunga is a rat just like them."

"Well, maybe something will happen," I said. "Maybe Fligh will cancel his invasion plans. There's still a couple of days yet."

"Maybe," Bunga said. "Anyway, Bunga feel better after talking. No decision, but feel better. Now sleep."

Bunga went through the little door into the passenger section. In a minute I could hear his mighty snoring.

I tried to think about Bunga's problem. I had an idea that I might be able to talk him out of invading Timor by reminding him that he had promised to help me before he'd promised to help Fligh. That might work; then again, it might not. It was hard to predict what Bunga was going to do. I couldn't think what *I'd* do if he decided that he had to invade Timor after all. My mind kept wandering. All I wanted to do at the moment was fly the plane and forget about everything.

Everything settled down into the easy kind of flying that makes you feel like you're standing still. Clouds were blanketed out beneath us, and the Crumbling Moon was low in the sky. It was perfect and starry. I thought of the sign of the Qris—for the first time in weeks, really. It had almost stopped having any reality for me. It had almost become nothing but something to sing about. But now it all came back—the golden yellow light, the hissing sound, the way I'd felt when I had seen that strange comet cut the moon in two. I touched the needle.

"I *will* deliver this to the Sultan of Equator," I whispered to myself. "I promise."

"The sultan knows that, my son," an old voice said softly, close to my ear.

I looked into the calm old face of Bapak Joya. "Shhhh! Let us speak quietly so the others may rest—we have a hard journey ahead of us."

There was something very strange about the old man. I really didn't know who he was, but I felt that I could trust him completely. It felt good to have him sitting up in the cabin with me.

He looked out at the starry sky. "A star for every wandering bark," he said to himself. He was quiet for a while. Then he sighed, "Ah, Java Jack! You have suffered much in your search, have you not?" He chuckled and patted me on the shoulder in a grandfatherly way. "I have also suffered in *my* search. No sooner would I find a trace of you when, presto, you were gone! Island-hopping, hunting for Equator. Then fame! Television, agents, bodyguards, reporters, crowds—all preventing me from getting to speak with you. It has been nearly impossible for me to complete my mission—to find you and bring you in secret to the island of Equator, before it is too late."

My head was spinning. My mouth hung open, and I couldn't get a word out.

Old Bapak Joya smiled. "It is not too late yet, my boy. Your mother and your father send you their love and best wishes."

Here I'd spent all this time looking for the island of Equator, and now, suddenly, the island had found me—had been looking for me all the time in the person of this kind old man. I started crying.

The old man patted me on the back. Through my sobs I managed to ask, "What course to Equator—which way do I steer?"

"The same as for Maggasang," Bapak Joya replied. "The island of Equator is not very far away from there."

21 "NOW WE HAVE arrived at the island of Equator," Bapak Joya said.

"But that's Maggasang!" I said. "I recognize Mount Gunungan!"

"I told you that Equator was nearby."

"But, Bapak Joya, I don't see any other island," I said.

"Java Jack, look at my face," the old man said. "Tell me, do you trust this old man?"

I looked at Bapak Joya's face. I did trust him. I knew that there was nothing harmful in this old person. I knew he would never lie to me or harm me. "Yes, I trust you," I said.

"Then do as I ask, without question. Fly down into Gunungan's crater."

"What? Are you crazy? That's an active volcano!"

"No, I am not crazy. And yes, it is an active volcano —but I give you my word that we shall not be harmed, and fifteen minutes after we descend into the crater, you will see your father alive and well."

I had no reason to do what the old man asked—no reason other than his mild and earnest manner. I could see with my eyes that Gunungan was nothing more or less than a volcano. The thirty-mile-wide crater was covered with clouds as usual—but what was beneath the clouds? I had a mental picture of fiery lava, smoke, and sparks. At best, even if the entire crater weren't a burning hell, we'd probably crash in the dense clouds and never be found.

Knowing this, it was surprising that I obeyed the old man, and put the DC–3 into a curving descent.

As we entered the clouds I said once more, "Bapak Joya, are you sure?"

"Yes, Java Jack, I am sure."

We came out of the clouds, and I saw that the crater was filled with water—a crater lake. The clouds created a sort of wispy lid to the crater top, and far below the water was calm and deep blue. In the middle of the lake was an island—perfectly round, with two smoking volcanic cones in the center. It matched the picture of Equator that Munah had drawn on her batik map.

Bapak Joya read my thoughts. "Yes, Munah's map was

accurate, although the land and sea route to Equator is not easy like this. Munah is my daughter, you see, and she copied the map I had drawn, which I in turn had copied in a time when airplanes were not dreamed of."

I set the plane down in a little harbor made by two long projections of pink Maggasang marble built out into the lake.

By this time Bunga and the rest of the crew had awakened and were staring out the windows in amazement. They wanted to know where we were.

"Oh, Bapak Joya thought we might like to stop en route and visit this place," I said. "It's a very interesting little island called Equator."

There was considerable whooping and cheering and screaming on board *The Flying Boogeyman*.

"Oh, yes, and another thing, Bunga—I want to mention it now before the sultan and my parents meet us and all the confusion starts. You've been kidnapped. You can't get away from here except by airplane, and I won't take you—and if Benjie tries to take you, I'll stick him with my needle. So forget about invading Timor."

"Well," said Bunga, "if you kidnapped, you kidnapped, so make the best of it. First time anybody tough enough to kidnap the Batik Pirate."

I taxied the seaplane up to one of the long stone wharves, and Bim jumped out to tie her up. A gang of people who had seen the plane come in were waiting on the beach, and among them I saw my mother and father.

They were standing with a guy I recognized at once. He was even taller than Bunga, and had war paint on and feathers in his hair. It was that same Dyak that Fligh had tried so hard to kill with his machine gun when we'd raided the village in the Cessna.

"That man," said Bapak Joya, "is the Sultan of Equator."

The wharf was narrow, so the welcoming committee stayed on the shore and the boogeymen, Bapak Joya and his servant, and Benjie the spare pilot made a dignified procession from the plane to the land. I did nothing of the sort. I ran so fast along the stone wharf that I practically flew—right into the arms of my mother.

There was a whole lot of crying and kissing and hugging and how-de-do and handshaking and more hugging and laughing and hollering. After a while, everybody was laughing and crying and talking at the same time. It was a wonderful, crazy time we all had standing around there.

Finally my father said, "Hey, I'll bet none of these cool-cats have had any breakfast. Come on up to the house. I've got a bunch of neat-o blueberry muffins just baked, and more where they came from."

My father was a real cornball. I had forgotten that. It made me happy.

We all followed my father and mother and the Sultan of Equator inland, giggling and slapping each other's backs, and hugging each other and carrying on like maniacs.

22 WHEN I GOT up close and saw the sultan, I realized that he, not Dr. Jeff Robinson, was my father. I looked exactly like him, except for the blond hair.

"Who is my mother?" I asked. This surprised everyone. They were planning to explain everything to me, and I'd sort of jumped the gun.

Marie Robinson spoke. "Jack, you have to understand that we all love you. You have always been with people who love you. We pretended you were our son because there was real danger from the sultan's enemies. Aunt Amy, back in Neosho, isn't really your aunt. She's your grandmother."

"Where is my mother?" I asked.

"She is lost inside Gunungan," the sultan said.

"You mean she's dead?"

"No. She is alive. I feel this very strongly," the sultan said. "She was lost inside the mountain many years ago, at a time when I brought five blindfolded holy men here to participate in a secret ceremony."

"The story Fligh's father told!" I said. "Old Gon the Dyak witch doctor!"

"Yes, he was there," the sultan said, "and Bapak Budhi Joya, the Buddhist teacher. The other men are all dead now. It was at that time that your mother wandered into the tunnel to the Fiery Star and was lost."

The Fiery Star—that sounded familiar. Where had I heard about it? Yes! The story Munah had told me. The story about the Invisible Hunter. Hadn't she said that the race of giants who once lived on Earth had left to go to a fiery star?

All this amazing conversation was taking place while everybody sat around eating blueberry muffins made from a packaged mix that had probably sat on a shelf in Singapore for ten years. We were in my parents' apartment, which happened to be in the Water Palace. The Water Palace was like an island within an island, floating in the middle of a pond in the middle of Equator.

"Years ago," the sultan said, "my wife, May Ackerman of the United States, and our friends, Jeff and Marie Robinson, came back to Maggasang with me to help my people find a better way of life. The local witch doctors as well as the smugglers and pirates didn't like me as a sultan. They preferred the old kind of sultan—fat, lazy, and corrupt, like—forgive me—your grandfather. Not many of the people were interested in the modern ways we wanted to introduce. Most of the ones who were are now living here in Equator. This island was unknown until old Bapak Joya found an ancient manuscript that told about it. Either nobody had ever bothered to climb to the top of the volcano, or, if they had, the ring of clouds that always obscures the peak prevented them from seeing anything.

"Bapak Joya translated the old manuscript and told me about it. It told of the secret network of tunnels under the Water Palace, and it described the ritual involving the five holy men. I decided to revive the ritual, and to move my residence to the Water Palace, once the home of sultans of Maggasang in the days of the giants.

"In order to enter the secret underground passages, it was necessary to have a special needle, one made of a substance called Qris. This material is not metal, nor is it of plant or animal origin—but it has properties of all three. It is made of an ore derived from meteors, like the magical krises of ancient times.

"The ancient writings told that such a needle could be found in a copper box hidden in the Water Palace. We found it, and with it we opened the stone door to the inside of the mountain.

"While I was engaged in the treasure room, your mother wandered away. I thought she had gone up, into the air. When the ceremony was finished, I led the five blindfolded holy men out. As soon as we had come back into the air of this world, the door shut behind us. Then I realized that your mother had not come out, but must have wandered farther into the mountain, to the tunnel to the Fiery Star that the old book spoke of.

"As soon as I could, I hustled the holy men off the island—all but Bapak Joya, to whom I told everything that had happened. It was impossible to open the stone door, as your mother had the needle with her. The only way we could get in to find her was to make another.

"Bapak Joya's wife, Ibu, had made magic krises years ago. She had stopped at Bapak Joya's request, because he doesn't approve of magic. Still, she was the last human being on Earth who knew how to extract and prepare Qris—the only one who could make such a needle.

"Ibu's ancestors had been rulers of Maggasang, and she agreed to make the needle, but only on condition that when I received it I would agree to marry her daughter, Munah.

"Now, a sultan may have as many wives as he wishes, but I never wanted any wife but your mother, whom I love very much. Still, I agreed to her condition.

"To prepare Qris takes years, and hundreds of steps, each of which must be performed perfectly. Once the Qris is prepared, it takes at least as many steps to make the needle. What is more, Ibu insisted that everything be done in a traditional, magical way. For example, a pirate from the sky had to turn up to deliver the needle, and although a map could be given to him, he could not be told the real location of Equator, which was less than a mile from Ibu's hut. That is where you came back into the story, my son.

"What is more, Bapak Joya, who is something of an astrologer, is sure that only on one particular date can we succeed in reaching your mother, wherever she is within the mountain—and that date is tomorrow, so your arrival is perfectly timed."

All this was more than a little confusing to me. To begin with, finding out that the people you have always thought of as your mother and father are not, and finding out that your real father is a sultan with feathers in his hair—not to mention all the rest—all this has to be upsetting.

It wasn't upsetting to Bunga and the rest of the

boogeymen. They loved a good story, and if it involved someone they knew, it was even better. They had listened to what the sultan—my father—had said with expressions of pure delight.

The rest of the day was given over to talking and asking questions. Bunga told about my exploits as a pirate, making them sound a lot more heroic and exciting than they were. I wanted to know all about my mother (the real one), and I wanted to know all about what my other parents, Jeff and Marie, had been doing all these years. And I was sort of fascinated by my new, real father. On top of all this, the people of Equator wanted a Boogeyman concert—it seemed that they weren't as isolated as all that. In between all the talking and carrying on, we ate all sorts of food that the people of the island brought us.

By night my jaw hurt from talking, my ears hurt from listening, my head hurt from thinking, and my stomach hurt from eating.

 23 THE WATER PALACE was a floating, artificial island in the middle of a pond. In the middle of the palace, which would have looked like a big wheel or doughnut if seen from the air, was an open place, like a courtyard, except it was water. In the middle of that open space there was a round, smooth platform of stone—another island. The stone platform had a large blue dome above it, supported by seven columns that were made of some kind of clear crystal. This was where the door to the inside of Gunungan was located—on an island inside a palace that was an island in a pond on an island that was in a lake inside a volcano—which was on an island.

It was seven-thirty in the morning. Everybody was there—on the edge of the moat that separated the blue-domed platform from the rest of the Water Palace. Ibu and Munah had arrived. Ibu was all dressed up—she looked like a queen—and Munah was beautiful. They smiled at me, but didn't say anything. My father was there—the sultan—and Jeff and Marie Robinson, whom I still regarded as my father and mother. That was strange, because I felt that the sultan was my father too, and I really already loved my mother, May Ackerman, who was supposed to be trapped inside Gunungan since I had been a tiny little baby. I'd been shown all sorts of snapshots of her. She looked a lot like Aunt—that is, Grandma Amy back in Neosho.

Bunga and the boogeymen were all lined up, and Benjie the spare pilot; and a lot of the people of Equator were there. It was all sort of dignified and formal, like the opening of a new bridge or something. Everybody had put on their best clothes, or spiffed up what they had by borrowing this and that from the Equator folk. Bunga had gotten hold of an enormous turban with a feather, the kind you see in movies.

My father, the sultan, made an announcement. It was a dazzler:

"My people, in a short time I will open the door to the inside of Gunungan and go to find my wife. Before I do this, I wish to make it known that I hereby abdicate as your sultan."

There were a lot of gasping sounds. Even in the short time I'd been there, I'd been able to see that the people really loved my father, and depended on him to lead them.

"In my place," he went on, "I appoint Bapak Joya as sultan—and Ibu shall reign as queen of this island with him. Now," he said to Ibu, "let your daughter marry whom she chooses."

Ibu looked really surprised, but she managed to maintain her dignity. Munah just blushed and looked at the ground—but that may have been because Bunga was staring at her and twiddling his mustache and smiling like mad. Old Bapak Joya looked unconcerned about the whole thing, as if to say, "You appoint me sultan? Okay, I'll be the sultan. After all, the Buddha has taught us that all life is an illusion. One role is as good as another."

Then there were a whole lot of people solemnly shaking hands and bowing to one another and congratulating one another. Practically everybody there had to shake hands with everybody else. I found this part of the morning a big bore. I wanted to get on with opening the door to the inside of Gunungan. I had already made up my mind that I would go inside with my father and help look for my mother.

I glanced at my watch. Seven-forty-five. The date was the eighteenth. Wasn't something supposed to happen on the eighteenth? Oh yes, Bunga was supposed to invade Timor while Fligh went after the treasure of Maggasang. I smiled to myself. After searching for Equator, which was where the treasure was, for months, we had only found it because Bapak Joya had led us there. I wondered if Fligh had given up, or if he was going after the treasure in some out-of-the-way place, only to discover that there was no treasure to be found.

I became aware of something spattering against the dome, like hailstones.

The planes were too high for us to hear the explosions of the machine guns—we just heard the whistle and thump of the bullets. Then we could hear the rat-a-tat, and the drone of airplanes. We looked up. Through the ring of cloud that rested on the rim of Gunungan's crater lumbered two strangely painted B–17s. I could see the flashes of the guns, and I could almost make out the comic-book-style paintings on the wings.

Fligh had arrived exactly on schedule.

 24 "QUICKLY! QUICKLY!" MY father, the sultan, shouted. "Everybody get under the dome. The bullets cannot reach us there!"

There were crystal stepping stones leading to the platform, and we scurried across. Lots of people just dived in and swam to the safety of the dome. Fligh's planes made two passes, spraying bullets, but nobody got hurt. Then the planes turned and disappeared through the clouds.

"They land someplace now," Bunga said, "or jump out with parachutes. Pretty soon they come back. We better get ready to fight."

Five or six of the sultan's soldiers had rifles, and Bunga and the boogeymen had knives and krises and a couple of pistols. The buildings of the Water Palace were mostly open-sided, and what walls there were were flimsy things made of bamboo and woven leaves and such. Anyone could shoot a bullet in one side of the place, and it would come out the other—if it didn't hit anybody. There was no place to hide.

"Jack, use the needle!" my father said.

He pointed to a little copper plate set in the middle of the stone floor of the platform. In the middle of the plate, which was carved to show the familiar rainbow-and-comet design, was a little pinhole. I understood what I was supposed to do. I pushed the needle into the hole, and turned it like a key.

I had wondered where the door to the inside of Gunungan was. The whole floor of the platform under the dome was smooth. Now I found out. There was a rumbling, grinding sound, and the floor began to split in two. People jumped this way and that as the crack widened beneath their feet. The sides of the platform swiveled out over the water. Steep stone steps carved out of solid rock showed wet and gray in the morning light.

"Everybody down inside," my father ordered.

We all lined up and started down the stairs.

The stairs were narrow and we could only go one at a time. When my turn came, after feeling my way down the dark passage for a while, I became aware of a glowing light beneath me. As I descended, the light got brighter. Then I saw a room—it was more than a room, really, sort of a high-domed cavern piled high with thousands and millions of jewels! The light I saw was just the trickle of daylight that made its way down the long stairway, reflected and magnified by the heaps of diamonds, rubies, emeralds, sapphires, and lots of other stones I didn't know the names of. It had to be the biggest treasure in the world!

"This good," Bunga said. "This best thing pirate ever saw. So much treasure here, Bunga too impressed to even feel greedy. This here worth the trip, even if Fligh kill us all."

"Fligh will not be able to kill us," my father said. "The stairway is too narrow for more than one person at a time. We can hide behind the piles of jewels and deal with each of Fligh's scoundrels as he comes."

"But what," said Jeff Robinson, my other dad, "what if they just decide to wait us out? We could starve down here."

"That's true," the sultan said. "But if Fligh knows enough about the legend of this place, he'll know that the doors may close by themselves. Without a needle of Qris, he can never open them. Of course, if he doesn't know that . . ."

"Then we'll all be trapped down here," I said.

"Look," Bunga said, "Bunga has been pirate for long

time. Let Bunga give you some good advice how to fight this fight. Everybody hide behind piles of treasure. When Fligh and bad guys come, let first one come all the way down stairs. Then let him have good look. After that throw jewels at poor devil—chase him upstairs. Don't shoot—don't kill. First poor devil tell other crazies upstairs what kind treasure down here—then nobody able to think. All Fligh and his buddies can think is, 'We gotta get that treasure.' Then they all swarm down here, and we get them one at a time." Then he said to Munah, "Don't worry, Bunga see that you not get hurt."

It was as good a plan as any. We decided to give it a try. After all, Bunga had the most experience in fighting.

It didn't work.

When Fligh and his army of F.I.M. maniacs and a few bad Dyaks and some assorted criminals and mercenaries arrived, they all came swooshing down the steps in one great tumbling rush.

The Equator people, hiding behind the piles of gems with some of the biggest and heaviest stones—ones as big as baseballs—in their hands, were taken by surprise. All of a sudden there was fighting everywhere.

It was too crowded and confused for any shooting. It was fists and krises and hurled jewels in the weird glow of the treasure. It was like fighting inside a bowl of Jell-O.

The boogeymen got organized first. Bim and Junah and Yudis, krises in each hand, formed a triangle, back to back, and held off a gang of Fligh's men. Bunga was in a corner, protecting Munah, and slashing right and left.

The sultan's soldiers were whacking away with their gun butts.

Everybody else was throwing jewels like mad. The jewels were the best weapons. They were hard and heavy and sharp-edged. I got hit in the leg with one by accident, and it really hurt.

I had my needle out. As usual, it was impossible to do any real harm with it, but it was working like mad, fending off Fligh's men, disarming them, exhausting them, setting them up for the boogeymen and the Equator people to capture them.

Bapak Joya and Ibu had set up a prison for the captured ones. They simply buried them up to their necks in jewels, with the help of a couple of strong Equator kids, and then stood over them with diamonds the size of coconuts in case they tried to move.

It looked to me as if we were winning.

But I hadn't seen Fligh himself. Tsang and Mambo had turned up, and had been promptly beaned with gems and dragged off to be guarded by Bapak Joya and Ibu—but no Fligh. I recognized Tolitoli Tim and Borneo Bill; they were giving the boogeymen a hard time. Still I didn't see Fligh.

I looked around for my father, the sultan. He was far back in the treasure chamber with his back to another doorway, swinging with both hands. I guessed that he was protecting the entrance to the tunnel to the Fiery Star.

Just then Bunga shouted, "Java Jack! Look up!"

I looked. There was Fligh. He was clinging to the

ceiling like a lizard. He hung on with one hand and was blasting away—in my direction—with a big .45 pistol. He laughed. "Where's your blue dress, Blue Blossom?" He peppered away in my general direction. One of the bullets hit the tip of the needle. It left a mark, but didn't bend it. The slug ricocheted off and hit a sneaky Dyak in the toe.

Bunga was battered, and his batik shirt was torn and stained with blood. Junah was limping, Bim's left arm hung loose, and Yudis was battling with one hand and holding his forehead with the other.

Jeff, my other father, had worked his way to the sultan's side. "Pull back to the door down here," the sultan cried. "We can hold them off forever!"

"Forever! Hah!" Fligh mocked. He came loose from the ceiling and came flying down like a bat, with his black cape billowing behind him. Under the cape he was mostly naked, and his tattoos glowed in the jewel-light.

On the ceiling of the treasure chamber, in the place where Fligh had been hanging, I saw a bundle of long red sticks attached to the stone with gray gooey clay. Dynamite. The long dangling fuse was spitting sparks.

"Forever?" Fligh cried. "Yes, you will be buried forever when the dynamite goes off!"

Fligh didn't intend to sacrifice himself—just his enemies and friends. This was clear to us because Yudis emptied his own gun into Fligh's body with no effect at all.

"Nothing touches Fligh!" Fligh cackled. "I am immune to bullets!"

"Dyak magic," Bim moaned.

Bunga gave me a terrible push in the direction of the sultan and the doorway. "You go with father," he grunted. "Go, go!"

Just as he pushed me, and I began to cartwheel toward the open passageway, Fligh made a vicious dive for me. The needle caught him right in the heart. It sank in and Fligh made a noise like a punctured tire.

Horrified, I struggled to my feet and drew out the needle. Fligh fell back—dead. As he sank backward his tattoos came to life. A python unwrapped itself from Fligh's body and slithered away. The dragonfly that had been on his back flapped its wings and circled the room, then slowly flew up and out the stairway to the island above.

All this happened in a moment. In the same moment, there was a blinding flash, and a feeling of pressure— then darkness. The dynamite charge had gone off.

25 ONCE AGAIN I had the experience of noticing how things seem to slow down sometimes, when really they are happening very fast.

When the dynamite went off, I was plunged into darkness. At the same moment I had the idea that Gunungan was erupting—along with the dynamite explosion. I thought I saw a shower of jewels and sparks and red-hot lava shooting upward.

I felt myself being buried under tons of gems and rock. Buried alive.

At the same time—while feeling buried alive—I also felt myself falling—flying, almost—through tunnels, through space.

I heard myself calling out. My voice sounded far away. I called to Jeff and Marie Robinson, who had been my father and mother for so long. I called out to my father the sultan. I called to Bunga.

And—this is strange—most of all, I was calling to my real mother, May, who had been lost inside the mountain so long ago. I was calling out to someone I really couldn't remember as I fell, tumbling and tumbling, through the darkness.

There was nothing to do but let go. There was nothing to do but fall and fall and fall in the dark.

"Mommy! Mommy! Mommeeeeeee!"

26 AND THEN, THERE she was. My mother. She looked just as she did in the photographs I'd been shown by Jeff and Marie and the sultan. She was sitting on a ledge overlooking a place that had to be another world. Actually, she wasn't sitting *on* the ledge—she was sitting upside down *under* a ledge of rock. I was sitting next to her. Why didn't we fall off?

In the distance I saw two suns, one bright and one dim. The sky was pink and streaked with gold. This had to be

Mars or someplace like that—but how had I gotten here?

"My goodness, you startled me," my mother said. "And you look just like . . . just like my husband . . . but your hair is yellow. Who are you?"

"I'm your son. I'm Jack. I've been looking for you for such a long time," I said.

"But that's not possible," my mother said. "Jack is just a tiny baby."

"I'm Jack," I said. I was totally confused, but somehow very comfortable, sitting upside down in this weird place with my mother whom I hadn't seen since I was a baby. "Have you just been sitting here all these years?"

"Years?" my mother said. "I've only been here for a couple of minutes. I was with my husband, the Sultan of Maggasang, and I wandered away from the room with all those jewels and came through this door . . . and . . . Oh yes, the door closed and I couldn't get back. So I sat down and waited for him to come and find me. It's strange, telling you this—it seems as though it happened a long time ago, and yet I'm sure I've only been here a couple of minutes."

"It hasn't been a couple of minutes, Mother," I said. "It's been years, and I'm your son, half grown up, and Father has been trying to make his way back to find you all this time, and he almost did, but there was an explosion, and, somehow, I fell into this place . . . and . . . Do you have any idea where we are?"

"You know, dear . . . that's strange, calling you dear, and here we've just met this second . . . I really do feel as though you were my son. . . . You know, dear, I haven't the foggiest notion of what this place is. I've never seen anything like it, have you?"

"Do you know that we're sitting upside down?"

"Why, so we are! Isn't that unusual!"

My mother appeared to be annoyingly slow-witted. But it wasn't just that she was dumb and didn't notice things. It was something else. It was as though she had a hard time being very interested in anything that happened. She just seemed content to sit there, upside down, and take it all in. I know she felt that way because I was beginning to feel that way myself. I was trying hard to be excited about being in this incredible situation, and finding my mother, but I just felt sort of sleepy and peaceful.

I was curious, and I said something sort of cruel, just to see if my mother would respond. "My father, the sultan . . . he was in the explosion. I think he's probably dead."

"Oh. If that's so, I don't suppose he'll be coming to find me after all," was all my mother said about it. Then she sat for a while—probably the equivalent of a year on Earth—and next she said, "You know, I love your father very much."

Well, at least she'd decided that I was her son. I was making a tremendous effort to take an interest in things. I just didn't feel it was right to sit there so calmly, the two of us. I had a pretty good idea that I was dead—although I didn't want to think about it—and I was worried that I didn't feel more upset.

My mother was perfectly happy to just sit there without saying anything, so I had time to think my own thoughts. I tried to get worked up about being dead—if, in fact, that was what I was. I tried to think of people I should be missing, like Jeff and Marie, and Aunt Amy—that is, my grandmother—and Bunga. But I couldn't get myself to really miss them. When I thought about each of them, I felt all this happiness and love—but I didn't feel bad.

Being dead was boring—but I couldn't manage feeling bored. I was thinking, all right, but I had the vague notion that I could dispense with that any time I wanted to and I wouldn't miss it, either.

My mother must have been reading my thoughts. "Yes, dear, it is very strange, isn't it?"

Then we sat for a while—maybe a minute—maybe an hour—maybe a year.

Then my mother spoke again. "How funny! Upside down in another world. Why, it's better than *Alice in Wonderland,* don't you think?"

I made one last try. "Look, while we're sitting here, talking about *Alice in Wonderland,* my father is probably buried by the dynamite or the volcano, and Maggasang is probably sinking into the sea, and—"

I stopped. It was foolish to get so upset. There wasn't anything we could do about any of that stuff.

"Jack, dear, do you have any idea why we don't fall off this ledge? It seems we should, being upside down—don't you agree?"

I shifted around and tried a handstand, which put me in a right-side-up position. It was easy and it didn't feel any different. Still, I felt a sort of pull of gravity—but somehow I wasn't heavy enough to be pulled down by it. I felt as though I *could* fall off the ledge if I really tried. It was like being an ant on Earth. They can walk any which way. Gravity doesn't seem to affect them much. Maybe in this world we were as tiny as ants.

27   "SORRY TO KEEP you waiting!" a big voice boomed.

The whole universe shook. We saw the pinkish ground far below us cave in.

The caved-in crater resembled a gigantic footprint. But where was the foot?

"Oh, I forgot—you can't see me," the voice said.

Another canyon caved in beside the first one. Then we heard a resounding crack that made us jump.

"My knee always does that when I bend down," the voice said. "Just hold still, and don't wriggle when I pick you up. I'm going to put you on my shoulder. Just hang on to a couple of my hairs so you won't get bounced off when I walk."

I tried not to wriggle in the invisible giant's fingers, but they hurt something awful. I groaned. Mom was lying flat on her back in the middle of empty space. She had to be in the palm of the giant's hand.

We got plunked down on an invisible shoulder as big as a house, and we grabbed onto invisible hairs that felt like young trees.

"Hold on tight! Here we go!" the giant said. Somehow, up close to his throat, the booming voice wasn't as bad. Before, when it had been aimed right at us, it had been nearly unbearable.

Particles of what must have been dust—to the giant—rose up from the ground. I got hit in the head and yelled, "Ouch!"

"What did you say?" the giant bellowed. "Hey, cut that out—it tickles!"

Cut what out? All we were doing was digging our heels in so we wouldn't slide off. "Hoho haha heehee!" he laughed.

"Are you the Giant Guardian?" Mother yelled.

"Are you the Invisible Hunter?" I shouted through cupped hands.

"Me? Oh no. Not me! The Guardian is having his bath. He told me you'd be coming, though."

"He *knew?*" I shouted. "He knew who we'd be?"

"Not exactly," the giant explained. "He didn't mention your names, or say how many of you there would be, or anything like that."

I got the picture. It was not precisely my mother and I who were expected, just some tiny Earthlings of some sort.

"You brought your needles?" the giant asked.

"Yes," I said. Mother looked blank for a moment.

"Oh, yes," she answered at last. "The needle." She pulled out the original one.

"Good!" the giant boomed. "By the way, I forgot to introduce myself. I'm Raymond. I'm a go-fer. You know, go-fer this and go-fer that. Haha hoho heehee."

The giant was a real wit—at least he thought he was.

"I'm May—and this is my son, Jack. How do you do?"

"How-de-do to you too," the giant said. "It's not far now. See? There's the Guardian standing over there."

We squinted and waited for the dust to settle. We didn't see anything but endless miles of gold and pink mountains with blue ridges.

"Oh, sorry," Raymond said. "I keep forgetting we're invisible to you."

28 "THIS WON'T TAKE a minute," the Giant Guardian, the Invisible Hunter, said. "After the operation you can both be on your way."

Operation? My mother and I looked at each other. We were standing side by side on an invisible surface inside an invisible shelter that kept out the sand and wind, but didn't prevent our seeing the two suns slowly setting on the horizon.

"Where are the needles?" the Guardian asked. Mother and I gave him our needles.

The Giant Guardian held them in either hand. Each

needle stretched until it was almost a yard long.

Giant fingers pressed gently against my waist and pinned my arms to my sides.

Giant fingers raised the two needles high above us, turned them around and around, as if they were being cleaned by invisible tools, and placed them, points downward, right over our heads.

"This may tickle a little," the Guardian said. He knew how to use his voice for tiny folk like us. "If you feel like laughing, go right ahead."

The point of the needle penetrated the soft spot in the middle of my head. The instant it started to go in, my brain started to tickle. The needle descended very slowly. It wasn't scary. This giant was a great surgeon.

I couldn't contain my laughter. In a few seconds, I was laughing hysterically.

Click. The needle inside me made a sound like the opening of a lock. Snap! A zillion tiny specks of bright light sprang out of me and surrounded me like countless stars. I looked at my mother. She was surrounded by stars too. We looked as if we were wrapped in miniature galaxies.

"Aah, good," the Guardian said. "Just let me jot a few things down. I'm going to let go of you. You can move a bit if you like, but don't run away. We're not through yet."

We heard the sound of a giant pencil scratching. We turned around inside our starry cocoons.

"I've written down all the necessary particulars," the

giant said. "Now, May, your door is the fiery star to the left—the glowing pink sun. Jack, your door is the fiery star to the right—the gold sun."

"Door?" we asked. "Doors to where?"

"Doors to the outside," the giant replied.

"Outside?"

"Outside the material universe," the Giant Guardian said, "the place where humans go sometimes when they die. I've never been there myself, not being human. Giants and djinns and the creatures of this universe cannot leave it without being utterly destroyed—but for humans, some humans, it's just another door."

"Then we are dead!" I cried.

"Not yet," he replied. "I mean to say, you are both full of the energy and pressure you've drained off from the Earth. So you are still alive in the earthly sense. But once you pass through our suns and shed the power you've carried with you, you will be dead to this world and alive in the next."

"But I don't want to die!" I shouted. "I want to go back, and take my mother with me!" I jumped up and down, but the giant had me between his fingers again.

"You'll have to take that up with whoever you meet on the outside, Jack," the Guardian said softly. "I'm just doing my job. We've got to keep the suns burning, you know."

"No, I don't know!" I shouted. "What are you going to do with us anyway?"

"*I* am not going to do anything," the giant replied.

"You are the ones who are going to do it. You are the ones who came down the tunnel. You are the ones who carry the maps of the universe inside you—the maps you're wrapped up in now. Your maps contain the routes for your journeys. All I do is insert the key, unlock the maps, and confirm your direction."

"But what's all that about keeping the suns burning?"

"You and your mother don't need your maps anymore. Your maps contain the excess energy you've collected on Earth. When you go through the tunnels of our once-fiery stars, you will shed your radiant maps. That radiance will spark the stellar fires once more, illuminate the suns you see dying and dim before you, and perpetuate the life of our planets and people for ages to come. For this, we are all most indebted to you—and, of course, to the wisdom of Whoever Thought All This Up."

With that, the giant pressed the needles all the way down so that the ends were flush with the tops of our heads.

Mother and I spun round and round, faster and faster. Our spinning got so fast that we began to ascend from the operating table, floating up through a passage in the invisible roof of the shelter where the Giant Guardian had taken us.

We shot skyward. We penetrated the bands of force that bound the planet to its suns. We were drawn toward our separate stars—my mother to the big pink one, I to the gold one.

I heard a rushing, roaring sound behind me and

looked back.

I was leaving a wake of billowing fire. I was igniting the star as I went through it. The star was a tunnel. My starry cocoon was peeling off, galaxy by galaxy, as I sped toward the end of the tunnel.

 29 OUTSIDE THE MATERIAL universe.

Outside everything.

Outside everything I ever thought there was.

I haven't got words to tell what it was like. All the words I've got are inside this universe, and all of them are about things that can't get out of it.

All I had ever read or thought or heard or imagined about heaven and hell, time and space, life and death, other worlds, other planes, other dimensions—all of it— all of it was stuff that was still stuck inside this material universe.

It was all stuff you can find with your mind or your heart or your star map somewhere in some corner of this big, this fantastically big universe.

My mother and I went somewhere beyond—outside all that.

I can't say what it was like. All I can say is that once I was there I definitely did not want to leave it. The last thing I wanted to do was to go back inside the material universe.

I never would have, but my father was there, waiting

for us, when we came out. He had some plans for me.

My mother and father were awfully happy to be to-gether again, and I was happy being with them. And in that place, wherever we were, outside the material uni-verse, it was possible to be happy in a way so much beyond what I'd always thought of as happiness. It was *some* happiness.

Then my father talked to me. He had an empty mayon-naise jar in his hands. He borrowed my needle, which was around my neck again, and poked holes in the lid while he talked. It was the sort of jar I used to catch things in back in Neosho.

I remembered catching caterpillars and watching them on my windowsill, spinning their cocoons. I remembered the shock I got one time when I woke up and found a rainbow butterfly in place of the brownish gray cocoon that had been there the night before.

My father said that I was going to go back. Back inside.

He said he understood my wanting to stay outside. He said that he would find it hard to go back too. He and my mother knew a lot about this place, this outside, even though my mother had arrived at the same time I had, and my father, who was alive and well in the fight in the jewel chamber, couldn't have been there much longer than us. The fact was, I really didn't understand too much about the place, while my parents seemed to know all about it, and acted as if they'd already been there forever. In a way, that was the best argument for what my father was saying—that it wasn't really time for me to be there yet.

My father told me that I should try to remember, after I went back inside, what it was like not having to think with a brain, or feed my stomach, or wait for whatever I was doing to get done.

I felt like arguing. "But if I go back, I won't recognize anything! Maybe it will be a million years later. Maybe there won't be any Earth left!"

My father laughed. "Remember when you used to put caterpillars into a jar like this?" I did—and so did he, although he'd never been in Neosho to see me do it. "Imagine that you are in a cocoon inside this jar. If you were also still inside the material universe and wanted to get back, let's say to Maggasang from the Fiery Star, it could take millions of years. But you're not in the jar, and you're not in the material universe. You've stepped outside for a while. Time and space and all there ever was for you is like the cocoon in the jar. You can carry it with you wherever you go. You can even unscrew the lid and put your finger right on the point of the cocoon from which the caterpillar—you—started spinning. You can put your finger on any point after that, including the point at which you left and came here."

I understood what he was saying, which is strange, because I can't really understand it now—I only remember it. Also, he wasn't really talking to me in the normal way, and it wasn't really a mayonnaise jar. That's just as close as I can come to describing what was happening.

"Maybe I could go back at a time a little later than the point at which I left," I said. I was remembering the explosion, the roof falling in, being buried under stuff.

"Son, it's really distasteful going back inside, no matter what point you go back to—but it only feels that way while you're here. Once you're back inside, life there will feel more real to you than life here—even though the opposite is true. Look."

My father unscrewed the top of the jar and took out a movie. I don't know how he did it—and there wasn't anything as primitive as a screen or a projector. He just produced a movie for us to watch.

It was a movie of the old life. The life inside the universe. The life on Earth. In Maggasang.

"These are movies that have just been made," my father explained. "In the making of movies, many more things are photographed than will actually appear when the film is finished. Some things are left in and some are thrown out. In the movie we are watching now, the director hasn't decided yet which scenes need to be filmed over, and which scenes to keep. And the ending hasn't been decided on either, so several versions are being filmed. It's a movie called *The Batik Pirate,* starring our old friend Bunga the Bugis."

My mother and father and I watched some of the life movie of Bunga. Bunga was crawling toward the star tunnel door. He'd had the wind knocked out of him. He didn't make it. A piece of falling rock crushed him. He died.

There was another version. Bunga crawled to the door. He saved Munah from being crushed. Together they reached the starry night. A rainbow arc of jewels and lava was spurting across the sky. The dome in the center of the Water Palace caved in. Bunga and Munah struggled to escape over the collapsing ground. They made their way to a boat and floated out to sea. Maggasang sank.

"It looks so real," I said.

"It is real," my father said, "it just isn't final." He showed more movies. There were all kinds of possibilities—all kinds of endings.

I began to understand what my father was trying to tell me.

"I'd like to see the movie called *Java Jack*," my mother said.

We watched my whole life movie. The ending was missing.

Now my mother told me that she wanted me to go back inside. "Go back and be a good Java Jack," she pleaded.

"But what's *that*?" I asked. "It's just a name I got called by Fligh."

"But it's already quite a name!" my mother said. "A pilot, a pirate, a singer, a son of a sultan! Think what you can do with your part in the movie from this point on! I'm so anxious to see the next scenes!"

I could see that they were going to have their way—and they were right, of course. I was going to have to go back inside. It made me sad.

"I think it's wonderful that you brought me here to meet your father," my mother said. "I don't think I could ever have found him without you." She patted my arm. "And isn't it nice to know where we are and that we're happy? You won't have to worry about us when you go back."

"And now you know in advance where you have to go when you have to go," my father said. "That will be an advantage."

I hugged them both and kissed them for the last time. We didn't cry.

I stood on the lip of the mayonnaise jar. I waved good-bye. I jumped.

The last thing I saw was my father screwing the lid back on and poking a few more holes in it with the needle.

To let in a little more air, I thought.

 **30** "THROW HIM IN jail!" Bunga bellowed. "He's no good. Maybe better kill him quick so no more magic, no more Free Island crazies, no more hurting people!"

Bunga paced back and forth in front of Fligh.

Fligh was on his knees. His hands were tied behind his back. Junah was holding on to his hair so he wouldn't try any tricks. Bim's arm was in a sling, but he was carrying a machine gun. Yudis and Jeff Robinson came rushing into the living room of the big mansion—the Maggasang Observatory.

"The eruption's stopped, Bunga!" Yudis shouted.

"It's incredible!" Jeff panted. "Incredible! One moment the mountain was spitting up and the next it was sucking in!"

"What do you mean?" Junah asked.

"Equator—the lake—everything! Gunungan gobbled it all back down!"

I could imagine it. It must have looked the way it does when you run a film backward. It must have looked funny.

"And now it's stopped," Jeff panted. "It's quiet as a graveyard."

"But it's all gone," Yudis went on. "The inside of the crater is just a big gravel pit, and the mountain is dead —no smoke—nothing."

Munah and Marie had come into the room.

"It's sad," Marie whispered. She held Munah's hand. "Equator was such a beautiful island."

Munah smiled. "No, I think it is better—better there are no more secrets. No secret islands, no secret treasures, no secret—" She stopped in the middle of what she was saying. She looked over to where I was lying on the floor behind Fligh. I was all wrapped up in burlap bags. I must have looked like a sack of potatoes. Nobody knew I was there. And I couldn't talk yet. I was still speechless from the shock of coming back inside.

I'd come to something like consciousness only to find myself just where I'd been afraid I'd be—buried under rocks and rubble.

Somebody was tearing away at the rocks above me. Digging. Blinding bright morning light hit me, but I couldn't close my eyes or even blink.

My eyes adjusted to the light. Whoever had found me was madly scraping away the rest of the debris that held me down. It was Fligh.

His face was sooty and scratched and bruised. His mouth was open. He'd lost a couple of his perfect teeth. The ones he still had didn't seem to glow anymore. His eyes were bloodshot. He looked a wreck. He looked good. He looked human. He took a deep breath and bent over and laid his ear against my chest. His fingers, all rough and torn up now, pressed on my wrist, searching for a pulse.

He must have heard something or felt something, because he started clawing away again at the rocks that covered my legs.

"I knew it! I knew—I knew you weren't dead!" he mumbled.

Tears were streaming from his bloodshot eyes. "I'm sorry, really I am." He cried like a little kid. "I'm sorry, Java Jack. I'm sorry. Come on now, don't die. I know you're alive. Please don't die."

It was a different Fligh. He went on mumbling and crying like that until he'd gotten me unburied.

All this while, Gunungan was going off like the Fourth of July. We were practically in the middle of it.

Fligh dragged me up into the light. Then he carried me in his arms. All I saw was blue sky streaked with smoke. Clumps of hot lava flashed by. Still, it was a beautiful sky, and I was glad to see it again.

Fligh laid me down and washed me off with cool water.

He scrambled around and gathered up leaves and flowers and stuff and pasted them onto my wounds with wet mud.

Somewhere he found some burlap sacks and wrapped me up in them, cushioning me with grass and leaves.

Then he picked me up again and carried me. It seemed like he carried me for a long time. Most of the way he was climbing and stumbling. Finally he hit some sort of path. He must have been exhausted, but he kept going.

At last he came to a place where I could hear voices, people shouting, sounds of hurrying.

I gathered that there was an evacuation going on. People were worried that there weren't enough boats to get everyone off Maggasang. Gunungan was going to *really* erupt, burst wide open, and everybody was trying to organize an escape before it was too late.

The Maggasang Observatory was evacuation headquarters. Fligh carried me right inside, and was promptly put under arrest by Bunga.

Then Gunungan changed its mind.

And Munah noticed the lumpy bundle Fligh had brought in.

"Bunga, what is that bag?" she asked.

"Fligh carry it," Bunga replied.

"What is it?"

I wished I could have said "Hi!" and seen the expressions on their faces, but I couldn't talk yet.

It took me a few days to recover the use of my body.

After that, I was good as new.

 **31** SOME OF THE people of Maggasang had managed to get themselves evacuated before the mountain went cold. Bapak Joya and Ibu were among those who had left. Bunga had put them on a boat with a pocketful of jewels, and eventually they landed in Singapore.

They decided they liked it there, and left the government in Munah's hands—so she was Queen of Maggasang.

The first thing she did was pardon Fligh. Then she had Tsang and Mambo kicked off the island, and she declared an amnesty for all the Sea Dyaks and mixed-up kids who'd taken part in the raid.

There were quite a number of jewels lying around the island, even though Gunungan had swallowed the bulk of the treasure. There were enough in the royal treasury to put the island on its feet in the way my father and mother and Jeff and Marie had always wanted.

Maggasang was in the news because of the eruption, and it wasn't long before word got out that the Boogeymen were there. Then we got lots of long-distance calls from booking agents and such, asking if we wanted to do a concert in Singapore, and did we have any new songs, and all that sort of nonsense.

The Boogeymen had a meeting and talked things over. Bunga was trying to think of something to do with all his pirates—I mean the entire Bugis fleet, which had turned up in the harbor. They didn't know what to do with themselves now that Bunga had left the pirate trade.

He wanted to get out of the music business too—he had decided that it was undignified. We agreed to give a farewell concert, a benefit for the victims of the volcano.

Maggasang immediately was mobbed with kids and reporters and television crews. We had the concert inside the crater of Gunungan—it was the only open space on the island big enough to hold everybody. It was a great natural amphitheater too.

The concert was a big success. It took three weeks just to clean up afterward.

Bunga helped Munah set up a trading company called Maggasang Mercantile, and together they set up a shipping company called Equator Line. That's where all the Bugis pirates came in.

Munah encouraged the people to set up farming and handicrafts cooperatives.

Yudis elected himself Minister of Education. Jeff worked with him. They were also making plans to build a city in and around the crater of the mountain.

Maggasang was turning into a busy place.

Junah stayed on as a singer—he'd always been the best one in the group.

Bim was Bunga's right-hand man in the new shipping company.

Jeff and Marie asked me if I wanted them to continue to be my parents. I said sure.

Everything was falling into place—and I was getting bored.

My grandmother, Amy, sent me a letter saying that school was starting soon, and did I plan on coming back to Neosho. I hadn't really thought about it, but when her letter came I realized that I missed her a lot. Never in a million years would she leave Neosho, so if I wanted to see her, I would have to go home. Besides, I sort of felt like going back to school with those same nonfriends I was used to.

Everybody in Maggasang was doing fine—they'd hardly notice I was gone. They were all busy and happy —except Fligh. He worried me.

Except for Munah and me, I don't think anybody had ever quite forgiven Fligh for what he'd done. That would take some time. And he refused to go away—he just hung around in Maggasang, looking sorry.

Bunga had always said that someday he'd go back to America with me, but right now he and Munah were very busy putting Maggasang on the map. They were pretty busy with each other too. I had the impression that Bunga pretty well fitted Munah's idea of the Invisible Hunter she had dreamed of seeing.

So it wasn't Bunga who went back to the States with me, in the end. It was Fligh.

Fligh was finished in Asia—at least for the present— and he knew it. Also, getting stabbed with the needle had changed him, as it had Bunga.

"I'm going to do penance, Java Jack," he told me. "I'm going to go to a university and become a doctor, and come back here and help poor people instead of hurting them."

We took the same plane to the States.

Of course, everybody in Maggasang said, "Java Jack, stay!"

But I really wanted to see my grandmother. I promised to come back to Maggasang, and I knew that the island of Equator would always be an important scene in my life movie, but it was time for me to go.

There was a big send-off at the airport. Suryo and Charma, the two pilots Fligh had kidnapped, came up from Surabaya. Old Huip did the food and drinks. Borneo Bill and Sulawesi Sue were bouncers in the Rumah Agung now. It was getting to be a high-class joint.

To the strains of "The Original Boogeyman Boogie-Woogie" we all said good-bye. It was like the last good-bye with my mother and father in that place outside the universe. We didn't cry. I knew I'd be coming back to Maggasang, just as I knew I'd be going back to where my mother and father were someday when the last scene in my movie had been filmed.

 **32** FLIGH GOT ACCEPTED at a midwestern university. Once Charlie and I flew the Cessna up to see him in Kansas City. He was doing fine. He looked so normal that I walked right by him in the airport. He didn't look like Fligh anymore. He wasn't called Fligh either. He'd changed his name.

I asked him how he'd chosen the name F.L.I.G.H. in the first place.

"The Fight for the Liberation of the Island of Gunungan Heaven?" Fligh chuckled. "Well, my old adopted father, Gon the *dukun*, used to say that heaven was what was inside the mountain. He might have meant the treasure—but maybe he meant something else." Fligh winked at me. I'd never told him about my trip outside the universe. I was actually beginning to think of it as a weird dream.

"You know, Java Jack, you ought to write down everything that happened to you while you were in Maggasang," Fligh said. "Because if you don't, someday soon you're going to look back on it and it's all going to seem like a dream."

He was still pretty good at reading my mind.

That was the last time I saw Fligh for a long, long time.

I'd gotten into the habit of wearing my Java Jack medallion.

One day one of the kids noticed it, and the name got spread around. It stuck.

I got along better with the other kids, and even made friends with two or three. I even showed them my room. They thought it was nifty.

Sometimes I'd wonder what my mother and father were thinking about the scenes they were seeing now in my life movie. Pretty boring business, it must have been. Every day the same scene—one day like another.

I was getting itchy feet. I'd written a letter to King Kanabombom asking permission to come to visit him in

Chatulistiwa and look for the Lost Valley of the Weebos. That was something to look forward to, but it was a long way off.

Then Mark Byrd, one of the kids I was friends with, came to see me one afternoon. He was all excited and hush-hush with this piece of old green and moldy leather in his jeans pocket. It had a lot of pinholes in it. It looked like the leather Gunungan Fligh had hung up in the cockpit of the Cessna.

"Java Jack, you're the only one who won't think I'm crazy. The other day I was hiking in the Ozarks up near Lake Noel, and I found this tunnel. . . ."

The hair on the back of my neck stood up.

". . . And there was this map carved on the hipbone of a skeleton inside—and I found this leather thing—and you can put it over the map—and I think it's got something to do with that old story, the one about the giant Pawnee hunter that nobody can see!"

Mark and I are planning to hike up there soon and see what we can find.